FALLEN

....

SHANGÉ AND MIJOGA

BY
MILTON J. DAVIS

To Ron,
Sword and Soul Forever!
Milton J. Davis
4/22/24

MVmedia, LLC
Fayetteville, Georgia

Milton Davis/MVmedia, LLC
PO Box 1465
Fayetteville, GA 30215
www.mvmediaatl.com

Publisher's Note: This is a work of fiction. Names, characters, places, and incidents are a product of the author's imagination. Locales and public names are sometimes used for atmospheric purposes. Any resemblance to actual people, living or dead, or to businesses, companies, events, institutions, or locales is completely coincidental.

Book Layout ©2017 BookDesignTemplates.com
Cover and interior art by Kristopher Michael Mosby
Cover design by Uraeus

Ordering Information:
Quantity sales. Special discounts are available on quantity purchases by corporations, associations, and others. For details, contact the "Special Sales Department" at the address above.

Fallen/Milton J. Davis. -- 1st ed.
ISBN:978-1-7372277-6-2

Contents

To those who fight for love

Love cannot be divided.

—Kenyan Proverb

SACRIFICE

Shangé opened her eyes to the gray rainy season sky. Something was different. She was not the same. She felt limited, as if her essence was contained. A sensation pressed against her being, a feeling she'd rarely experienced. But this time it felt . . . permanent. It was then it all came back to her.

She stood earthbound before the elders. They glared at her with their starlit eyes, their anger evident. She had gone too far. Mijoga stood beside her, his posture defiant. He had no idea what he faced. She glanced at his handsome umber countenance and remembered why she fell in love with him despite their differences. A wave of regret washed over her; her love had sentenced them to death. But at the moment of judgement, Mama intervened. Because of her interference Shangé still existed whole instead of scattered across the heavens. She could not say the same for Mijoga.

It took her a few moments longer to realize she was in human form. She stood then gazed on her body. She was naked, her dark brown skin slick with sweat. The sun burned despite the cloudy sky, an indication that this was early in the rainy season. She looked about but could find no signs of human settlements. She needed to find people soon, and she needed to arm herself. Mijoga taught her that people needed weapons to protect themselves from animals and each other. They did not possess the powers of the Sky Folk, as he called them.

Shangé shut her eyes, reaching out with her senses. She smiled; it was good that the Elders had not stripped her of all her talents. There was a settlement nearby. She would go there and hopefully find shelter and assistance until she could figure out what the Elders wanted from her.

She made her way across the savannah to the settlement. The grasslands around her teemed with wildlife, most of it staying away from her. It was a sign that they were familiar with humans, and their instincts told them to be wary. Shangé began to worry when her legs weakened and her stomach began to ache. She did not know what was causing her to feel this way. This was not her first time in human form, but it was her time remaining in such state for so long.

"Hunger," she said aloud. That was the reason for her weakness. She would have to find sustenance. She had no weapons and did not relish killing an animal. She would have to continue to the settlement and hope she did not succumb to her situation before she reached it.

Another sensation gripped her; one that was familiar yet unnerving. It emanated from behind her. Shangé turned toward the source, squinting her eyes to see. A creature loped toward her; its head lowered to the ground. As it neared Shangé could see that it was a simba, a large male with a thick mane. But there was something else about this simba. It raised its head and their eyes met.

"Mijoga!" she exclaimed.

The simba roared in response and increased its pace. Shangé ran toward the beast, her heart filled with joy. The Elders had spared Mijoga in their own way. Mijoga roared again and Shangé stopped. Mijoga was not greeting her; he was attacking her. She searched frantically for something to defend herself, hoping she would not have to use it. There was nothing. She looked up and Mijoga was upon her, leaping at her with paws wide and claws bared. Shangé jumped to the left almost too late. She screamed as Mijoga's claws ripped her cheek, the force spinning her like a toy. She hit the ground hard, the wind forced from her lungs when her chest slammed the hard earth. Mijoga bit her ankle and she cried out again. Shangé kicked with her free leg, striking Mijoga's nose. He let go of her ankle then backed away, shaking his massive head. Shangé drew her wounded leg close to her body as she held her damaged face with her hand. Mijoga crouched, ready to pounce.

"Mijoga, no!" she shouted.

Her voice struck Mijoga like a club. He stumbled back, his eyes displaying his confusion. The feline orbs shifted again; first registering shock, then recognition.

"Mijoga, it's me." Shangé extended her bloody hand. "It's me!"

Shame flashed in Mijoga's eyes. He let out a mournful roar then fled.

"Mijoga, no!" Shangé called out. "Come back!"

She tried to stand, forgetting about her injured ankle. The pain forced her back to the ground. The combination of agony, fatigue and hunger was too much for Shangé. Her eyes rolled back and she passed out.

* * *

"Wake up, daughter."

It was not her mama's voice, yet Shangé opened her eyes. The woman leaning over her smiled then nodded her head.

"Good. Good. We thought we were going to lose you."

"Where am I?" Shangé asked. It hurt for her to speak.

"You are in my village," the woman said. "We heard your struggle with the simba and we came to help. We thought you were dead, but Naserian noticed that you were still breathing."

"I thank you," Shangé replied. The mention that she almost died sent a chill through Shangé. If she could die, she was truly human. Her exile was more serious than she had imagined.

"What is your name, aunt?" Shangé asked.

"I am Kioko."

The woman reached for Shangé's face, pulling back the cloth that covered her wound. She frowned.

"What is it?" Shangé asked.

"Your wound will heal, but the scar will remain," she said. "If only we had reached you sooner."

"I am not concerned about that," Shangé replied. "Kioko, what happened to Mijo . . . the simba that attacked me?"

"The hunters tracked it for a time, but it evaded them."

Shangé sat up. Her head spun for a moment then cleared.

"I must find it," she said.

"I would think you would never want to see it again."

"It is special to me."

"It tried to kill you."

"It was confused," Shangé said. "It belongs to me."

Kioko hesitated before answering.

"I will send for Lemuani. He will know what to do. I will also get you some clothes."

"Thank you," Shangé said.

Kioko brought her garments before sending her daughter for Lemuani. By the time the man arrived others had gathered at Kioko's hut. They gossiped among themselves, cutting glances at Shangé as they spoke. Shangé ignored their rudeness; she was only concerned with finding Mijoga.

The people parted and Lemuani entered the room. The elderly man walked slowly, supporting himself with a stick carved in the shape of a twisting serpent. A ragged gray beard covered his face, his rheumy eyes shifting about suspiciously.

"Kioko, why have you summoned me?" he asked. "I have better things to do than . . ."

His eyes met Shangé's and his mouth formed a circle. He fell to his knees and touched his forehead to the dirt.

"Spirit, forgive me!" he said. "I was not told of your presence!"

The others repeated Lemuani's gesture. Shangé felt awkward; she no longer deserved their respect.

"Please rise," she said. "Lemuani, Kioko said you can help me."

"What do you wish, Spirit?"

"I need to find the simba that attacked me."

"Do you think that is wise, Spirit? An animal that can hurt you is a dangerous beast."

"It is not an animal . . . at least not completely," Shangé said. "We are bonded. It just doesn't know it yet."

"I will send for Olamayian and Mingati. They are our best simba hunters."

"This is not a hunt," Shangé said. "Make sure they understand."

"I will, Spirit."

"And do not call me Spirit. My name is Shangé."

"Yes . . .Shangé."

Lemuani hurried from Kioko's house, the others close behind. Kioko moved away from Shangé, fear on her face.

"Do not worry," Shangé assured her. "I once watched over humans. I won't hurt you."

Kioko smiled. "You can't. You still need rest. It will take time for Lemuani to contact the hunters. They are in the bush. Until then I will help you heal."

"Thank you, Kioko."

"No, thank you, Shangé. I am honored that you chose me to help you. The spirits will surely favor me for it."

"I cannot speak for them, but I will always be in your debt."

It took three days for the hunters to arrive. Shangé healed quickly, another sign that the Elders did not strip her of all her abilities. She spent the time learning tasks from Kioko and the others. She didn't want to be helpless.

It was a rainy day when the hunters arrived. Shangé was learning to make bread when they called out, asking for permission to enter Kioko's home. The duo dried themselves as much as they could, then prostrated before Shangé.

"Spirit, we are proud that you have summoned us," Olamayian said. He was the taller of the two, with a chubby face and broad shoulders. Mingati squatted beside him, looking at Shangé directly. He didn't seem as impressed with her as Olamayian.

"I thank you for coming," Shangé said. "I hope you can help me find the simba that attacked me."

"We are the best simba hunters in the village," Mingati said. "We will find your simba and bring it to you."

"I'm going with you," Shangé said.

"A simba hunt is a dangerous thing, Olamayian said. "It is no place for the inexperienced."

"You forget what I am," Shangé said. "I will go with you."

"And what weapon will you wield?" Mingati asked. "Will you protect yourself as you did before?"

The scars on Shangé's face itched after Mingati's words. Her eyes narrowed and the hunter took a step back, his hand tightening on his spear.

"I was caught off guard," Shangé said. "I was hungry and tired. This time, I will be ready."

"We will be honored to have you with us," Olamayian said. "The rain will hinder us, so we must wait until it clears."

The men stood to leave Kioko's home.

"You can stay here," Kioko said. "It's dry and there is plenty of food."

"That is not necessary," Mingati replied. "We have provisions, and we are used to being in the rain."

"I insist," Kioko said.

"We both do," Shangé added.

"Thank you!" Olamayian replied. Mingati's response was less enthusiastic. Kioko made them stew and the four ate while Olamayian entertained them with stories from the bush. Mingati sat silent, never taking his eyes off Shangé. His suspicions were warranted, but Shangé did not have the time or temperament to relieve him of his doubts. All she could think about was Mijoga. She would not wait for the rains to cease. She decided she would leave to find him in the morning, with or without the hunters.

Grey clouds muted the rising sun. Shangé and the hunterss emerged from Kioko's house, Shangé leading the hunters to where she encountered Mijoga. The men searched about the area, studying the grasses then looking into the distance.

"I see no signs," Mingati said. "Are you sure this is the place?"

"I am," Shangé replied. "I think I would remember where I got these."

Shangé touched the scars on her face and Mingati looked away.

"I'm sorry, Shangé," he said. "I apologize for my callousness."

Shangé nodded. She relived the moment in her head and fought back a shudder.

"This is not simba habitat," Olamayian said.

"It is no ordinary simba," Shangé replied.

"Yet it is a simba. There are some instincts that it will follow. It has no choice."

Olamayian set out at a trot, Mingati following. Shangé ran with them. She kept up with the tempo, despite the hunters' pace and distance. As they neared a river bordered by low bushes and trees, Olamayian raised his hand.

"Do you hear it?" he asked.

"Yes," Mingati replied. He looked at Shangé with worry on his face.

"I think we have found your simba."

The men ran again and Shangé followed. As they neared the river a wave of fury overwhelmed her and she stumbled. The hunters continued to run, oblivious to her plight. The fury that overtook her transformed into familiarity.

"Mijoga!" she shouted.

Shangé sprinted by the hunters, snatching Mingati's sword as she passed him. She neared the river and saw what caused her fear. Mijoga stood in the middle of the shallow waterway surrounded by male and female simbas. His mouth hung open; his breathing heavy. One of the male simbas lunged at Mijoga and he sidestepped as he slapped its face with his paw. The simba's head jerked and it fell into the water. Another simba, a female, used the distraction to close in on Mijoga and nip at his hind leg. Mijoga spun and he roared. He bit at the female, but she retreated too fast.

"Mijoga!" Shangé shouted. She high stepped through the water and broke through ring of simbas, stopping before Mijoga. Mijoga roared and charged her.

"Mijoga, it's me, Shangé!"

Mijoga rose onto his hind legs, towering over Shangé. She did not move. If she was going to die, then so be it. She did not wish to live if this was their fate.

Mijoga dropped on all fours then stalked toward her. Their eyes met and Shangé dared to smile. The majestic simba pushed his head against her chest gently. Tears welled in Shangé's eyes as she gripped his mane.

"I see you," she said. "And you see me."

Mijoga jerked his head, tossing Shangé into the water. He blocked the simba lunging where Shangé had been with his body then wrapped his forelimbs around the beast. The two maneuvered their heads about looking for an opening to bite. Shangé scrambled to her feet, bloking the path of a female attempting to join the fight. She swung Mingati's sword with skillful precision, driving the female back. The other simbas gathered but Shangé held them at bay. One of the simbas decided to attack; its charge interrupted by a spear piercing its side. Olamayian and Mingati appeared, shields raised and spears thrusting at the pride. The simbas fled, each familiar with the hunters and their deadly skills. Shangé didn't notice their arrival; she embraced Mijoga.

"I know this is not how we envisioned being together," she whispered. "But you are alive, and I am thankful for it."

"Shangé?"

Olamayian and Mingati stared at her and Mijoga.

"This is your simba," Mingati said.

"Yes," she replied.

"What will you have us do?" Olamayian asked.

A strange sensation entered her mind. Shangé raised her head to the sky. Clouds formed overhead, but these were not rainy season clouds. It was something more ominous.

"Leave. Now," she said. "The Spirits are coming, and it is not safe for you to be here."

The men backed away, then turned and ran.

Mijoga pressed against her, a rumble coming from deep in his throat. Shangé massaged his mane.

"Don't worry," she said. "There is nothing we can do. Let us hope whatever they do to us, it will be quick."

The clouds pressed together then descended around them. The Elders were present, and they were not pleased.

"Why is he still alive?" they said in unison.

"Because I chose to spare him."

The clouds shifted and a being emerged, one Shangé loved more than any other.

"Mama," she whispered.

"You defied our judgement," the Elders said.

"As is my right as Eldest," Mama responded "Mijoga did nothing to deserve death."

"He defiled a spirit."

Mama looked at Shangé.

"It was my daughter's transgression. What mortal can resist the attentions of a Spirit? She has been punished enough, and so has he."

Mama walked to Shangé and Mijoga then stood between them, placing her hands on them. Shangé felt her power and lowered her head in respect.

"Shangé and Mijoga will serve us," she said. "They will be our presence in this land. When our worshippers call, they will answer. This will be their penance until the Elders are satisfied."

Mama was answered by silence. The clouds ascended into the gray sky then dissipated, revealing the dim stars.

"We shall see."

Shangé hugged Mama tight.

"Thank you for saving us," she said.

"You are safe for now," Mama replied. "The Elders may decide to go against me if they can overcome their fear."

Mama pushed Shangé away at arm's length. She touched the scars on her face.

"These marks will remain until the Elders forgive you," she said. "They are a reminder of your disobedience. Serve us well, daughter."

"But what of Mijoga?" Shangé asked. "Will he ever be a human again? Will we ever be together?"

Mama's smile faded.

"In one life . . .or another."

A strong wind enveloped them and Mama's form dissipated like the smoke from a weak fire. Shangé gazed where she once stood for a moment, then knelt to hug Mijoga's neck.

"We are still alive, my love, and one day we will be together, in one life or another."

They walked together toward the distant hills, the sun's light fading until they disappeared into darkness.

MWANAMKE TEMBO
(THE ELEPHANT WOMAN)

For six months of the year Kiswahili, Arab and Indian dhows sailed east with the monsoons, their cargo holds pregnant with the goods of East Africa. Six months later they returned, their African bounty exchanged for eastern luxuries and ready to begin the cycle again. The Mombasa merchant Belay played both sides of the coin like most Swahili traders. One particular item whose value spread beyond Africa was ivory. The tusks of the massive tembos were prized throughout the trade lands for its beauty and versatility. It was a common item of trade, its value fluctuating with supply and demand. This particular season ivory was invaluable for it was nowhere to be found.

Changa was assisting the bahari make repairs on Belay's dhows when the messenger boy found him. The boy trembled as he took in the imposing presence that was Changa Diop, former pit fighter now merchant apprentice.

"Changa, bwana Belay wishes to see you immediately!"

Changa strode to Yusef, who sat on the docks raising his beer gourd to his lips. Changa slapped the container from his hand.

"Come with me" he ordered.

"Where are we going?" Yusef slurred.

"To see bwana Belay. Pretend you're sober."

They followed the boy to Belay's home. The old merchant paced the floor in the lower level, mumbling as he was prone to do when he was agitated.

"Bwana, you sent for me?"

Belay jerked his head toward Changa and smiled.

"Ah, Changa! Come, I have a special task for you."

Belay's smile dissipated when he noticed Yusef barely standing.

"Is he drunk?"

"No, bwana," Yusef slurred.

"Get out!" Belay shouted.

Yusef bowed and almost fell into Belay. Changa caught his big friend and spun him towards the door.

"Wait for me outside," he whispered.

Belay glared at Yusef until he exited.

"I would toss him into the streets if it wasn't for you," he said. "Why do you tolerate him?"

Changa shrugged. "He's a good man. You won't find a harder worker or more loyal man in Mombasa."

"When he's sober," Belay added. He sat at his desk. "I need you to take a safari into the interior. The Omani want ivory and there is none. My suppliers are very late with their delivery."

"How soon do I need to leave?"

"As soon as possible," Belay replied. "If the Omani can't get ivory from me, they'll sail down the coast to Sofala."

"I'll make arrangements immediately," Changa said as he stood.

Belay came to him, placing a fatherly hand on his shoulder. "Do not fail me, Changa."

Changa returned the gesture. "I won't, bwana."

* * *

Changa was ready to depart within a week. His crew consisted of eighty men, sixty bearers and twenty warriors. They departed Mombasa at first light, making good time despite their provisions and trade goods. Belay had given Changa much responsibility on the safari, more than he'd done in the past. He had the merchant's permission to negotiate for the precious material at the hunting camps. It was a test of Changa's merchant skill and he was eager for the opportunity.

The safari also offered a useful reason for Yusef's participation. Changa's looming friend was Kikuyu and knew the way to the tembo hunting camps. It saved them the expense of hiring a guide, which thrilled Belay immensely. The bulky man stood before the group, his fists pressed into his hips, a scowl on his face.

"Come on, dogs!" he shouted. "The sun slips away. We have miles to cover an ivory to claim!"

Changa shook his head. "Calm down, Yusef. These men are porters, not slaves."

Yusef huffed. "I've seen better men feeding vultures."

"Grab your gear and let's go," Changa said. "Like you said, the sun slips away."

Their departure did not go unnoticed. Any plan by Belay drew attention, especially from his competitors. His domain was the sea, so the inland excursion drew much curiosity. After a brief stop on the docks to secure additional supplies, they entered the mainland. Years had passed since Changa journeyed into the bush and he was overwhelmed by the plethora of wildlife inhabiting the savannah. Yusef strode ahead, a huge smile on his face. He turned to Changa with sparking eyes.

"This is my home, kibwana. This is the land that made me." He slowed, walking stride for stride with Changa.

"I'm saving my cowries to purchase one hundred head of cattle and grain to plant my fields. I'll build a farm outside my home village. When I become wealthy, I will take many wives from the best families who will bear me sons."

"That's a bold future coming from a man who loves beer as much as you."

"Make fun of me while you can, kibwana," Yusef snapped. "I would break your thin neck if I didn't respect you."

Changa smirked. "Lucky for me. Just keep focused on our task."

They came across the first village two days later. The chief, Kiamboga, was a short, thick man with bulbous cheeks. He offered them food and rest, but Changa's impatience would not allow it.

"We seek the tembo hunters," Changa said.

The chief nodded. "As do we. In normal years our men would travel to Mombasa with tusks from the hunters. They are not farmers so they trade with us for food, milk and meat. But they have not come. The men we sent to contact them have not returned."

"You have no idea what happened to them?" Changa asked.

Kaimbogo shook his head. "Like I said, we are not hunters. They could have been killed by Maasai or simbas. Who knows? Their families mourn and I can do nothing. We will send no more men. The money we make from the tusks is good but not necessary."

"Is there someone that could lead us to the hunters?" Yusef asked.

"Of course," Kaimbogo answered. "But they won't. You are a good group of warriors but my people are tired of disappearing."

"I will show you."

Changa and the others sought the owner of the female voice that volunteered. She knelt, her head partially bowed as she looked at them. Wide brown eyes scanned them then lingered on Changa. She lifted her head, her pretty face evident to all.

"This is not your place!" Kaimbogo said to the woman.

"My husband is gone," she countered. "If you will not find him I will."

She stood then approached Changa. "I am Kenda. I will take you to the tembo hunters."

"No!" Kaimbogo protested. "You will bring her wrath on us, too?"

Changa placed puzzled gaze on the chief. "Her? Kaimbogo, what is going on here?"

Kaimbogo glared at Kenda before responding.

"The people call her Mwanamke Tembo. They say she is the reason the ivory has stopped. Some say she has killed the hunters because they slaughter her children."

Changa frowned. "And you believe this?"

Kaimbogo shrugged. "All I know is the ivory supply has ceased and my men have not returned."

"Maybe there is a war in the interior," Yusef offered.

"That could be," Changa answered. "It wouldn't be the first time war interrupted good trade. Still, bwana Belay has given us a mission and we must complete it."

Changa extended his hand to the chief. "Thank you for your hospitality. I hope you don't mind if we allow Kenda to help us."

Kaimbogo waved his hand. "It's her fate, not mine. Not that I expect anything to happen to you, bwana Changa."

Changa chuckled. "Of course, you don't."

They left the village and set up camp. By nightfall they cooked bush meat over the campfires. Kenda sat at Changa's fire, her sad eyes gazing into the flames. Yusef plopped down beside her, a gourd of palm wine in his large hands.

"What troubles you, sister?" he asked.

Kenda's head snapped in his direction. "What do you think? My husband is missing two weeks now. I cannot manage our farm and raise my children myself. I must find him."

"Who manages it now?" Yusef asked gruffly. "Your man is gone and you are here. Who watches your children?"

Kenda slapped the wine gourd from Yusef's hand. "My family, stupid mbogo!"

Her anger faded as a worried expression marred her face. "If I can't find my husband, I can't keep my farm. My children and I will starve. If Kaimbogo wont' find him, I will."

"Your husband may be dead, Kenda," Changa said. "We won't know until we find the tembo hunters."

"Changa!" Yusef exclaimed. "Your words are harsh."

Changa shrugged. "There's no need to lie. Kenda knows this. That's why she's here."

Changa looked at the woman. Her wet eyes reflected the firelight as she turned away. Yusef scowled at him.

"Of course, we can't be sure until we meet the hunters," he added.

Kenda stood and stalked away from the fire. Changa went back to consuming his stew, ignoring Yusef's angry stare.

"You didn't have to say that," Yusef said.

"As I said before, she knows," Changa answered. "Either we will find him or we won't."

Kenda led them through the scrub forests and open land the next day, setting a pace that was difficult to maintain for those used to dhow life. They spent the night at the base of a wooded ridge, the men grateful, Kenda disappointed. The next day they scaled the hill.

"The hunters' camp is over the ridge," Kenda said.

They reached the summit by midday. Below them was the camp, or what remained of it. The huts were crushed, piles of grass and thatch surrounded by decaying bodies. Kenda let out a painful wail and scrambled down the hill. Changa and his men followed more cautiously. They entered the dead camp, their weapons at the ready.

"Search the area," Changa commanded. "Check the perimeter for tracks. Whoever did this much destruction had to leave a trail."

Yusef joined Changa.

"There was definitely a fight here," Changa said.

"And the hunters lost," Yusef replied. "Are we going to search for their killers?

"Of course not," Changa said. "I want to know how long ago this took place. Whoever did this might return. We don't want to be here if they do."

"Bwana, come quickly!"

Changa ran to the excited porter. He and three others gestured at a large ruin. Protruding from the pile were the tips of tusks. Changa moved aside the grass, exposing a wealth of ivory.

"It seems we have been blessed," he announced. "Whoever destroyed the camp didn't do it for wealth. They would have taken the tusks."

"It was probably Maasai," Yusef said. "They care for nothing but cattle.."

"Whatever the reason, there's more than enough ivory here for us to take back. We'll make camp in the hills just in case whoever did this returns."

Yusef gestured toward Kenda. She trudged from one body to the next, kneeling before and inspecting it delicately with her fingers, her lips moving with silent words.

"She won't find him, Changa said. "Even if he's here she won't recognized him. They've been dead too long."

"Maybe she can sense him," Yusef said. "He was her husband. They say that a woman and her husband have a special bond. We could help her."

"You can help her," Changa suggested. "I came here to find ivory and I have."

"We wouldn't have found it without her," Yusef argued.

Changa folded his arms across his chest. "That's true, but like I said, there is nothing we can do. He is lost."

Yusef grunted at Changa then joined Kenda."

"Let me help you," he said.

She glanced at him then continued her morbid inspection. Changa and the others went into the hills to set up camp. By nightfall they had eaten and retired to their tents. Sleep came quickly to Changa, his mind at ease. He had completed his first solo task for Belay.

Changa awoke suddenly; his hands seeking his sword. A feeling had seeped into his mind, the sense that something was coming, something ominous. Moments later the ground trembled beneath him. He jumped to his feet as the quaking increased. A sound ripped through the night, a sharp trumpeting that gripped his heart and pressed out a hint of fear. He exited his hut and was greeted by the worried stares of his companions. Yusef rambled to him.

"The ground shakes, kibwana," he said. "It happens here sometimes."

Changa didn't reply. His attention was drawn to a wavering luminescence rising over the horizon. The shuddering grew as the light came closer. The trumpeting increased, a sound heavy with warning.

"Tembo," one man said. "Something has frightened them."

"Or angered them," Changa added.

"Where is Kenda?" Yusef asked.

Changa scanned the camp. The woman was nowhere to be seen. Yusef must have done the same; for no sooner had Changa looked at his friend did he rush down the hill to the hunters' camp. Changa chased after him, followed by the rest of the men. The strange light increased, beams streaking through the trees and illuminating the camp. Changa emerged from the tree line and stumbled. A ragged vanguard of tembos advanced on the encampment. But these beasts were like nothing he'd ever seen.

Bleached bones pressed against their translucent hides, their trunks ghostly extensions from their heads. They followed the largest tembo, a massive matriarch whose trunk emitted the eerie blasts cutting through the humid night. Astride her was a woman. Scarification laced her face, lines that glowed with the spectral light of the herd. The tembo rider held a massive *shoka* in her left hand. She waved the weapon while screaming a sound similar to the matriarch.

Kenda stood before the charging herd, her face bunched in anger. She yelled at them, her voice drowned by their cacophonous stampede. The tembos halted before her, rising in unison on their hind legs. Yusef reached the woman and lifted her into his arms like an errant child. The tembo rider leaped from the matriarch, the shoka raised high as she plummetted like a bird of prey towards Yusef and Kenda. Changa rushed by the fleeing duo, raising his sword and knife above his head. The rider slammed into the three of them, pitching Yusef and Kenda forward. Changa caught the bit between his blades as the impact knocked him onto his back, his thick arms trembling to hold back the shoka. He stared into the malevolent eyes of the tembo woman. Her skin was grey like the ghostly animals she commanded, hanging loosely from her gaunt frame. She pressed the shoka down, the bit inching closer to his face. Changa had fought many adversaries but never had he experienced such relentless strength. This was a struggle he was sure to lose. Changa let his arms go limp as he jerked his head aside. The bit plunged into the ground inches from his face. He twisted his body, throwing the tembo woman aside. She rolled and sprang to her feet. She snatched her shoka free and attacked him again. Changa rolled and blocked, desperate for a chance to stand. The tembo woman was too fast.

The woman raised her shoka again and Changa heard a familiar yell. Yusef crashed into her and the two tumbled away. Yusef's advantage was temporary. The matriarch tembo's grey trunk struck him like a serpent, wrapping around his thick waist and tossing him aside like a twig. Yusef's diversion gave Changa time to stand but nothing more. No sooner had he regained his feet did the woman strike again. Her ghostly pachyderms attacked with her, flailing their trunks at him. Changa withstood the relentless pummeling as he concentrated on avoiding the woman's sinister shoka.

A roar split the ominous night and the tembos answered, trumpeting as they fell away. A simba leapt into Changa's sight, a full mane feline larger than any he'd seen. It drove the tembos back, swiping at their legs and trunks with no sign of fear. Changa raise his dented sword to deflect another shoka swing and was shoved to the ground. He looked up to see a different woman standing over him brandishing two swords.

"Nokofa!" she shouted. "This is not your realm!"

Nokofa, the tembo woman, backed away.

"Shangé?" Her eyes narrowed and she snarled.

"So, they send the fallen one to do their dirty work. You cannot help these violators. They would hunt until my children were no more. I will not allow that."

Nokofa raised her head and trumpeted. Her tembos swiftly formed behind her. She leaped backwards, landing on the head of the matriarch. Nokofa trumpeted again and the herd disappeared into darkness.

Changa finally had a moment for the strangeness of the night to settle. The simba strolled up to the woman called

Shangé, nuzzling against her thigh. She sheathed her
swords and embraced the simba, her arms disappearing in
his thick mane. She closed her eyes and smiled.

"Thank you," Changa said.

The woman stood and the simba crouched.

"No, Mijoga!" she ordered. Her eyes narrowed on
Changa.

"Leave now," she said. "Nokofa will return."

"We came for the tusks," Changa replied.

"Leave them. Nokofa will kill you if you touch them."

Changa hesitated, considering his words before answering.

"We can't," he finally said. "We came for the tusks and
we won't leave without them."

"Then she will kill all of you," Shangé said. She turned
to walk away but Changa grabbed her shoulder.

"Wait," he began.

Shangé slapped his hand away. Mijoga advanced towards him, a low rumble seeping from his bared teeth.

"Leave this place," she warned again. "Never come
back."

Shangé and Mijoga strode into the darkness. Changa
watched them disappear, his mind a jumble of thoughts
until a familiar moan reached his ears.

"Yusef!"

The burly Kikuyu lumbered out the darkness supported
by two comrades. Kenda walked beside him, her eyes staring into his.

"Are you okay?" Changa asked.

Yusef nodded then grimaced. "I'll be better in the morning. What just happened?"

"I guess we know why the ivory has stopped," Changa said. "We have intruded on a battle between spirits it seems. The tembo woman has declared war on the hunters."

"So, we go home empty handed?" Yusef concluded. "Belay will not be happy."

"Neither will I." Changa's face mirrored his disappointment. He would fail at his first task and he was determined not to, spirits or no.

"We'll rest tonight," he said. "Tomorrow I'll decide what we do."

The strange encounter did nothing to affect the camp's slumber. Snores, grunts and heavy breathing joined the sounds of night beasts among the dark hills and grassland. There was no such comfort for Changa. He sat at the fire, the glowing embers casting a faint light on his brooding visage. He wished a human war had been the reason for the ivory shortage. In war there was always someone more interested in themselves, some person willing to look the other way for the right price. But spirits had no price; they fought for their own reason, motives far beyond the comprehension of humans. He would have to find a way to circumvent Nokofa's anger and Shangé's warning. He had to get those tusks.

Something moved just beyond Changa's vision. He jumped to his feet, a throwing knife in his hand. Shangé and Mijoga emerged from the darkness.

"There is no way around us," Shangé said. "You should leave."

"I won't go without ivory," Changa replied. "Why should Nokofa or you care? The tembos are dead. Why should it matter if we take the ivory?"

"Because if do, others will want more and the hunters will coming back," Shange said.

"So, you agree with Nokofa?"

Shangé sat before the embers. Mijoga lay beside her, resting his massive head against her thigh.

"I do not care about the fate of the tembos. But Nokofa lives for them. She is their totem, the master of the place where their spirits rests. She has heard their stories of the hunters and it has angered her. She came to stop the killing, but that is not her place."

Shangé stared at Changa and he shifted. She seemed to be inspecting him, contemplating whether he was worthy.

"Since you will not leave, Swahili, maybe you can help me."

Changa was intrigued. "How?"

"I cannot defeat Nokofa alone. Mijoga is a noble companion but her tembos are too many. You and your friend may help reduce the odds."

Changa smirked. "Nokofa almost killed me."

"A lesser warrior would be dead," Shangé replied. "As for your friend, he's not as skilled as you, but he is durable. He may live long enough for us to succeed."

Sunlight brushed the eastern horizon. Shangé glanced at increasing light then stood.

"If you wish your ivory meet me at the hunters' camp at midday."

She reached into her waist pouch and extracted a small bag. She extended to Changa and their hands touched. Shangé's eyes widened, a smile coming to her face like the rising sun.

"It seems you hold your own secrets," she said. "The son of a kabaka is no ordinary man. You will make a strong ally."

Shangé's words distracted Changa, sending him back to a moment he'd buried away long ago. There was no time for memories; he had to concentrate on the task at hand.

"What is this?" he asked.

"Boil it and use the solution to clean your blades. It will help you against the tembo spirits."

Shangé and Mijoga stood then merged into the bush. Moments later the camp stirred. Yusef came to him, the big man rubbing the sleep from his eyes.

"Kibwana, did you sleep well?"

"I don't know," Changa replied. He looked at his hand; he still held the herb bag, a confirmation that Shangé's visit was not a dream.

"We should go home," Yusef advised. "The tembo woman will not let us collect the ivory and we are too few to hunt for it ourselves."

"I won't go home without the ivory," Changa countered. "Take this bag and boil the contents."

Changa handed Yusef the bag. Yusef looked at it suspiciously.

"Just do as I say," Changa scolded.

While the others went about their day, Changa waited for Shangé. He wondered how she knew of his past just by a touch and why it mattered. He was far away from that life, unable to return. Usenge took his father's life and sent him fleeing, his ruthless tebos hunting him for years. Yes, he was the son of a kabaka, but it had done him no good. He could never stand against Usenge, at least not alone.

Shangé and Mijoga emerged from the bush at midday. Yusef and the others rushed to Changa's side, weapons ready. He waved them down.

"Who is that?" Yusef asked. "Another spirit?"

"Yes," Changa replied. "But they are here to help us. Nafasi!"

A short muscular man with round cheeks and a serious face stepped forward.

"You're in charge until we return. Don't go into the camp."

"How long shall we wait for you?" Nafasi asked.

"Two weeks." It was a guess at the most.

Nafasi nodded and went back to his duties. Yusef and Changa ambled down the hill to Shangé. The woman looked them over and nodded her approval.

"It will take a week to reach Nokofa's refuge. I trust you told your people to stay away from the camp?"

"I did."

"Good, let's go." Shangé patted Mijoga's head and they jogged into the bush. Changa and Yusef followed. They ran the remainder of the day, stopping only when they could see no more. Shangé built a fire while Changa and Yusef rested, both men exhausted. Mijoga loped off into the darkness, returning later with an antelope between his jaws. He dropped the carcass at Shangé's feet then waited patiently as she cut a section for the three of them. The largest portion she gave back to the simba.

Shangé, Changa and Yusef cooked the meat over the fire. Changa stared at Shangé, wondering if he should ask the questions worrying him. She looked up suddenly and smiled.

"Ask your questions, merchant man," she said.

Changa cleard his throat before speaking.

"Why is mwanamke tembo killing the hunters?"

"Because they kill her spirit-children."

"Is she a tembo?" Yusef asked.

"No, she's not," Shangé answered. "She is the spirit that watches over them. She maintains the balance. The hunters were taking many, so she stopped them."

"And by doing so upset the balance," Changa surmised.

Shangé nodded. "Which is why I must stop her."

"Are you a spirit?" Yusef asked.

Shangé smirked. "Not anymore. I serve those who rule over us all."

Mijoga appeared. He lay before Shangé and licked his paws. Shangé massaged his mane and he rumbled in approval.

"I was once like her," she said. "Humans were my responsibility and I watched over them dutifully. Like Nokofa I came to care for them too much. A certain man drew my attention, the son of a chief whose spirit glowed like my own. One day he looked up into the stars and stared into my eyes as if he knew I watched him. He was so handsome; his body was strong like a baobab. His name was Mijoga."

Changa's eyes shifted to the magnificent simba. Mijoga glanced at Shangé and continued to rest.

"One day Mijoga called to me," Shangé continued. A little smile formed on her face. "I answered. We began to make love under the stars, exposed to the eyes of my own. No sooner did we touch that I was taken away from him. We were judged and condemned. Mijoga was to be killed; his soul cast into darkness, but my mother, the eldest of the spirits, intervened. She placed his essence into the body of a simba. I was stripped of my status, cast to the world as mortal. Though we were separated we eventually found each other."

"So why do you serve those who condemned you and your lover?"

Shangé's expression was muted. "Because it is all I know. I still hope that I will be forgiven. I may not rise again among the spirits, but they may at least grant Mijoga back his life. That would be enough."

They ran the next two days in tense silence, Changa barely noticing the change in landscape. Scrub brush and grasses melded into rocky soil and hills pockmarked by shallow lakes. On the third day, they covered less ground, slowed by the taxing terrain. On the fourth day Shangé finally broke the silence over a meal of wildebeest and yams.

"We are close to her," she announced. "We will attack at dusk."

"Why?" Changa asked.

"Nokofa cannot sustain her power all day. During daylight her tembos sleep. She summons them at sundown."

Changa nodded as he chewed his yam.

"You and I will confront her directly," she continued. "Yusef and Mijoga will deal with the tembos."

Yusef stopped chewing his meal, his mouth dropping open. "You want me to fight a tembo?"

"They are spirits. They require Nokofa's magic to exist. They will be weak at the most. Besides, you'll have Mijoga with you."

The simba growled at the mention of its name. It looked at Yusef with assurance in its eyes. Yusef looked back, shaking his head. Changa was concerned as well, but he had no choice. They had to trust Shangé.

"How will we do this?" he asked. "She is hard to kill."

"We can't kill her. She is immortal."

"So, what do we do?"

"Nokofa wears a talisman that gives her human form. If we can take it from her, she will revert to a spirit. She won't be able to harm us or them."

So there was a chance, Changa thought. "What it this talisman?"

"It is the leopard band around her head. It contains the gris-gris securing her in this world."

After another day of travel, they arrived in Nokofa's realm. Tall trees grew thick in the ash fed soil, blanketing mounds of earth that once spewed fire. Shangé stopped and shaded her eyes from the bright sun. She pointed to a cluster of stooped hills, each identical in height and width.

"There," Shangé said. "We'll find Nokofa beyond those hills."

Changa rubbed his chin to hide his unease. He recalled his last encounter with the tembo woman. Yusef looked at him, worry in his eyes.

"We should rest," Shangé finally said. "We'll need all our strength tonight."

Changa did not sleep and neither did Shangé. He watched her pace before the fire, her eyes watching the outline of the hills against the clear night sky. Occasionally she would peer at the heavens, her mouth moving but emitting no sound. Changa wasn't sure, but it seemed the stars shifted in response. He closed his eyes and tried to sleep. All he wanted was to bring back the ivory back to Mombasa.

Shangé roused them as soon as the sun descended below the hills. They climbed together, tracing a winding path to the hilltops. A pale-yellow glow radiated over the mounds, pulsing in time with a rhythmic voice rising over the trees. Dozens of feet below them a bizarre scene played out. Nokofa swayed before a chasm filled with countless tembo bones. Some bones were bleached white with age while others still carried the stench of death, grey flesh still attached to them. The tembo woman's chants were unintelligible to Changa, but they agitated Shangé. Her face bunched, her eyes narrowed.

"You and I will attack Nokofa," she whispered. "Yusef, you and Mijoga must work your way down to the chasm. Don't let anything emerge."

Yusef nodded, but his drooping eyes and downturned mouth expressed his misgivings. Changa had no time to reassure him; Shangé bolted over the hill and crept down toward Nokofa. Changa hurried to her and they worked their way through the sparse foliage together.

"Remember, our goal is the talisman."

Changa could see the strip of skin encircling Nokofa's head glowing with the light of the bone pit.

"Let's end this," he said.

Changa snatched a throwing knife from his sash, took aim and hurled it at Nokofa's head.

"No, Changa!" Shangé reached for his hand too late. Nokofa spun, batting the knife away with her shoka then leaped toward them. Shangé shoved Changa aside and Nokofa landed where he once stood, her blade splitting the ground. Shangé pounced, both blades flailing. Changa scrambled to his feet, sword in one hand, throwing knife in the other. He was sure Shangé's furious assault would give him an advantage. He was wrong. Nokofa slapped his blades away then swung the shoka at his scalp. He ducked, the blade passing inches from his head. Shangé and Changa's speed prevented Nokofa from attacking them but neither could penetrate her defense.

Something wrapped around Changa's waist, crushing the breath from him. He rose into the air, the pressure increasing. He looked down at the translucent appendage encircling him then up into the cold eyes of a resurrected tembo. He stabbed the nefarious limb and the tembo screeched. Changa fell, his dense body smashing into the foliage. He lay stunned, gasping for air when Yusef's face appeared above him.

"I'm sorry kibwana," he said. "There were too many of them."

A cacophony of trumpeting rose from the chasm. Nokofa manage to raise her minions despite Shangé's relentless attack. Mijoga dashed back and forth along the chasm edge, roaring, biting, and slashing at the hundreds of spectral tembos emerging from the pit. Yusef ran to assist him; Changa climbed to his feet and staggered toward the fighting spirits. Changa arrived too late. As he ran to Shangé, Nokofa's shoka slipped by Shange's sword and sank into her ribcage. Shangé's swords tumbled from her hands as she collapsed. Nokofa straddle her, the bloody shoka raised over her head.

"Why did you make me do this?" Nokofa shouted. "They condemn you and you serve them?"

"Because I must," Shangé replied.

Nokofa shook her head. "You always lived as a fool, Shangé. Now you shall die as one."

Changa threw his knife. It struck Nokofa's head, nicking the leopard band as it knocked her off balance. Shangé screamed as she jumped to her feet, wrapped her fingers around the band and ripped it from Nokofa's wounded head. Nokofa's eyes went wide, her angry yell dying in her throat as she faded away into a luminous smoke. The shoka fell as the essence that was Nokofa ascended into the sky. The ground jolted; Changa turned to see the tembo specters fall back into the chasm, their long dead bones animated no more by Nokofa's nyama. Yusef and Mijoga stared into the abyss for a moment, savoring their unexpected reprieve. The simba departed first, loping to Shangé. Yusef staggered to Changa.

"Is it over?" he asked.

Changa looked toward Shangé and Mijoga. "Wait."

Shangé raised her arms; her hands open to the sky. She chanted in a tongue unfamiliar to Changa, but her tone revealed the meaning. Brightness shifted in the sky then descended over her. Motes of light hovered then disappeared. Shangé fell to her knees, cradling her face in her palms.

Changa approached Shangé, placing his hand lightly on her shoulder. The wound Nokofa inflicted on her had healed. Shangé looked at him, tear stains on her soiled face.

"Go collect your tusks, Changa," she said. "Mwanamke Tembo will bother you no more."

"And what of you?" he asked.

Shangé looked away. "It seems my price is not paid yet."

It was not Changa's way to ponder about the spirits, but he was sure a wrong had been done. But there was nothing he could do. The ways of the spirits were beyond his understanding and control.

"Thank you, Shangé," he said. He turned to walk away.

"Wait." Changa turned, and Shangé offered Nokofa's leopard headband to him.

"Take it. It contains much nyama. It will add to yours."

"Mine?"

Shangé grinned. "You are the son of a kabaka. You were born with great nyama. You just haven't realized it yet."

Changa took the band. It vibrated in his hand for a moment then ceased. Shangé stood then gestured to Mijoga. The simba hurried to her side. Shangé patted Mijoga's mane and together they disappeared into the woods.

Yusef walked up to Changa. "Now is it over?"

"For us it is," Changa said. "Shangé's quest continues."

A roar echoed in the darkness and the stars above shifted.

"Come Yusef. It's time to go home." They walked together towards the peaks, a wealth of ivory waiting for them to claim. The darkness made it difficult going but they made it to camp by daybreak. The men looked grateful and relieved upon seeing them, especially Nafasi. He ran to Changa, grabbing his hand and shaking it furiously.

"Allah has spared you!" he shouted.

"Our return is due to other blessings," Changa replied.

Just then Kenda appeared. She ignored Changa, her joyful eyes locking on Yusef's battered bulk. She ran to him, brushing by Changa to stand before his friend.

"You have come back," she said, a tinge of relief in her voice.

Changa could not remember when Yusef had smiled so without a gourd of palm wine.

"Mwanamke Tembo will harass us no longer," Changa announced. "Tomorrow we will go to the hunters' camp and gather the tusks."

Nafasi looked concerned. "Bwana, there is too much ivory, more than we can carry."

"Yusef, you and Kenda will go to the village and hire porters," Changa said. "We will prepare the tusks while you're away."

Kenda struggled to hide her smile, but Yusef's emotions were obvious.

The men constructed huts for Changa and Yusef, although their energy for Yusef was wasted. No sooner had night fallen did Yusef steal into Kenda's hut. The sounds seeping through the woven branches left no doubt of their feelings for each other. Changa found himself sitting alone again before the fire, rolling Nokofa's headband between his fingers. Another object to add to his talisman collection, each one said to possess some power which added to his own. Changa smirked; this so-called nyama had not helped him so far. It did not help him prevent his father execution, nor did it help him avoid years of slavery. Still, there was something about the objects that made them worth keeping. Each represented a significant moment in his life. One day, when he was home again, he would tell his children the stories that brought the talisman to his hands. That day was still far away. For now, his concern was getting his tusks to Mombasa.

Fallen

WALAJI DAMU
(THE BLOOD EATERS)

Shangé crouched on the balls of her feet, her swords drawn. She stared into the thick brush, waiting for the sounds rushing toward her to make known their source. Whatever the creature was revealed to be, she knew why it was running her way. Mijoga had been hunting most of the morning and his persistence finally bore fruit. Fruit what kind, she did not know.

The bushes jolted, spraying leaves in every direction. The ground vibrated again her soles; whatever was coming her way was massive. Mijoga's familiar roar was answered by a husky bellow and Shangé's eyes widened. Mijoga was driving a buffalo toward her. She lost her rhythm as the beast rumbled side to side, dodging trees like a dancer and bringing down shrubs like a tembo. Its eye rolled with fear and pain then focused on her. A black mane rose above the foliage, Mijoga's roar bouncing off the trees. He had done his part, now it was her turn.

Shangé remained in the path of the charging bull, moving her lips and she silently counted. The bull was before her, its head lowered, its horns inches from her chest. Shangé jumped then twisted, landing on the bull's back.

She lay flat then reached down with both blades below the bovine's neck. In one motion she cut the bull's throat then sprang upward, somersaulting off the bull's back and landing on her feet. The beast crashed into a thick tree and tumbled sideways onto the grass. It shook for a moment then lay still.

Shangé sheathed her swords and approached the bull. A an odd rumble stopped her; she turned to see Mijoga stalking toward her, his ears flat on his head, his tail jerking threateningly.

"No, Mijoga," she pleaded. "Do not go. Do not leave me."

Her fears were coming true. Mijoga, the spirit of her mortal lover, was losing his struggle against the lifeforce of the simba he possessed. The creature approaching her did not see a companion; it only saw an object between it and its prey.

Shangé stared into Mijoga eyes and extended her ka inside him. Mijoga shook his head and roared, attempting to clear her from his mind. She continued to reached deep, searching for the essence she knew as Mijoga the warrior. She found it pulsing weakly, fading into the darkness of the simba's mind. She shared her ka, touching his waning spirit with hers. The union was orgasmic and exhausting. Shangé knew what she did was dangerous to her. Every contact with Mijoga drained her ka as well. She had already lost the strength to return to the heavens. If she continued, she would lose her ability to serve.

Shangé withdrew her ka, blinked and found herself staring into the simba's complacent face, his snout inches from her nose. He rumbled and licked her cheek with his rough tongue. Shangé grasped handfuls of his mane and shook his head from side to side.

"Stay with me, Mijoga," she whispered. "You will be free one day." She wished she believed her words.

Shangé set about the task of butchering the buffalo. Mijoga waited with human patience and was finally rewarded with meat. Shangé's respite would take much longer. After slaughtering the carcass, she gathered wood and leaves, constructing a smoker to preserve the meat. Toward nightfall she finally ate, enjoying the succulent flesh with wild yams and fruit. She was covered with blood and smelled of smoke. She remembered a lake nearby so she packed up the smoked meat and carried it to the lake shore. She stripped off her clothes and bathed, the warm water soothing her wounds and her ka. She washed out her clothes and hung them to dry then laid out her blanket on the soft grass. Her eyes searched the heavens, worry heavy on her mind. It had been weeks since she heard from the spirits. Ever since she fell from their presence and receive their sentence, they had demanded her service. But lately that demand had waned and it concerned her. She had not done enough to earn their forgiveness for she was still mortal and Mijoga was still a simba. A fearful thought came to her; had they abandoned her? If so, there was no hope for the two of them. Mijoga would eventually succumb to the nature of the simba and she would be alone.

There were others that could help her but they required a price she wasn't willing to pay.

"Go to the Land of Lakes," the voice in her head spoke. The command came so suddenly Shangé jerked upright and awoke Mijoga.

"The people suffer from an old foe," the voice continued.

"Who is it?" Shangé asked. There was no response.

Shangé wasted no time. She packed her belongings and supplies then dressed.

"Come, Mijoga. Maybe this time we will be rewarded."

* * *

The Land of the Lakes ran along a rugged valley sliced into the surrounding hills by a jagged celestial knife. The lakes sprawled among green mountains, huge bodies of water that held abundant fish and attracted large numbers of animals. The rivers that accompanied the lakes were violent entities, their swift waters often torn by large stretches of rapids that could smash the sturdiest canoes into splinters. The people of the land paid homage to both lakes and rivers; praising the lakes for their sustenance and fearing the rivers for their power.

Shangé emerged from her hut overlooking a wide river snaking between two huge lakes. For weeks she and Mijoga waited for the next instructions from the spirits but none came. She ambled to the hill slope, casting her restless eyes on the waterway below. Though signs of human life abounded, she had seen no one. She was beginning to wonder about the wisdom of the spirits when Mijoga appeared over the slopes, his actions speaking for him.

"Someone is coming," she said aloud. She joined Mijogo on the opposite side of hill. A procession emerged from the forest below. The participants wore simple clothing made from bark, their bodies covered by white chalk patterns. Two of the people, young bare-chested men with bird tattoos on their stomachs, carried a large bronze statute resting on a wooden platform. An old man led them, his body covered by a cotton blanket that brushed his bare feet. They chanted a song as they struggled up the hill, a melody Shangé was well familiar with. It was a plea for the spirits' assistance.

"Go to our hut," Shangé said to Mijoga. "It is best they do not see you for now."

Mijoga grunted his disapproval then sauntered away.

Shangé waited impatiently as they climbed. Her annoyance gave way to sympathy as they came closer. These were poor, fearful people. The statue they bore was probably an accumulation of their wealth transformed to an offering to insure the spirits' intervention. It was also a waste; whatever these people wanted would not be bought by any material offering.

Shangé was sitting when the pilgrimage reached her. The people kept their distance, their trepidation apparent in their averted eyes. The priest seemed just as afraid, his hands trembling as the bearers place down the idol.

"Great priestess," the priest announced with a quaking voice. "We have come to pay you homage as you requested. Please accept this idol as a symbol of our gratefulness."

As Shangé stood to inspect the idol Mijoga emerged from behind the hut. The people cried in terror and began to flee down the hill.

"No!" the priest shouted, his voice robust for an old man. Mijoga felt the nyama in his command and smiled. The priest was stronger than he looked.

Mijoga jogged to her side and she rubbed his head.

"Don't fear. He is my companion."

The priest nodded. The people returned to their positions, prostrating before her.

"Your gift is generous, but I do not need such reverence," Shangé said. "Tell me what troubles you."

The priest lifted his face then spoke.

"Three moons ago the ground shook. This is not unusual for our land is close to the gods and often feels their restlessness. What happened days later is what gave us dread. Our people began to disappear during the night, one by one. We would find them dead days later, the blood gone from them. We called on you for weeks once we realized our gris-gris would not protect us. Noe the people will not leave their huts. Crops die in the fields and the animals go unfed. No one has seen whatever it is that has caused this terror. The people have taken to calling it walaji damu, blood eaters."

Shangé did well to hide her puzzlement. She had lived countless years among the spirits and witnessed many strange and wonderful things among humans. Never had she seen anything like the priest described.

"What is your name, uncle?" she asked.

"Majambere."

"Take me to your village, Majambere. We will discover the cause of this hardship to your people."

Majambere's town was a modest gathering of homes crowded by the banks of a small lake. They were fishermen and farmers, their only livestock a small herd of goats. The villagers that had not come to the hill were hurrying to complete their chores, their eyes constantly darting to the darkening horizon.

"It is almost time," Majambere said. "The walaji damu will come tonight."

"How are you so sure?" Shangé asked.

"The moon will not shine tonight. They always come when it's darkest. That is why we came for you today."

Majambere's followers scattered as soon as they reached the marketplace.

"Hurry!" he urged. "Finish your tasks and get into your homes!"

"What will happen now?" Shangé questioned.

"They will go inside and lock their doors." The priest's face took on a dim cast. "I will hang gris-gris over their doors and chant for the spirits to protect us through the night."

Shangé knew the answer to her question before she asked. "Does it help?"

"For some," he confessed. "The walaji damu do not fear our gods."

Shangé patted Mijoga's head. "They will learn different tonight."

She pointed toward the homes. "Hide among the huts, Mijoga. I'll stay here in the market. If this thing appears near you, drive it to me. Hopefully it will choose an easier target."

Mijoga rumbled and trotted to the dwellings. The priest was still standing beside her, his eyes following Mijoga.

"He understands you?"

"He is not what he seems," Shangé said. "Go to your home, priest. We will handle this."

The priest bowed and scurried away. Shangé watched him until he was in his home then sat cross-legged in the center of the marketplace. She took out her swords and lay them before her then closed her eyes, extending her senses over the surrounding area.

The deep darkness of a moonless night descended on the village. Shangé kept her eyes closed, using her acute senses to track those moving through the night. The unusual quiet was a sign of strange things. Shangé sensed no movement other that herself and Mijoga, who paced restlessly among the huts. The prayers of the villagers drifted to her ears, the same prayers that once rose to her when she was among the spirits.

A celestial warning shattered her concentration and her eyes snapped open. An object dropped from above, hurtling toward her with amazing speed. Shangé grabbed her swords and jumped to her feet as the object landed before her. It was a being unlike any she encountered. Its skin was grey like ash, its wide head mounted on a short thick neck. It was blind, but its large ears and wide nose reveal it had evolved to its state. It held a crude spear with an obsidian point in its gnarled hand. Its mouth opened and a piercing sound cut into Shangé's head, staggering her. She stumbled away from the creature, its spear barely missing her throat. She threw up a sword instinctively, knocking the spear away. The other sword swing was planned. It sliced the creature's abdomen and it shrieked again before crumbling to the ground into its own guts.

Two more creatures landed before her, shrieking and thrusting their spears. Shangé blocked and dodged, amazed at their speed and strength. More creatures landed in the village, running to the huts. They were met by Mijoga, the simba charging from the darkness unperturbed by their sharp cries. Some of them broke away and attacked the huts but Majambere's magic held firm, at least for the moment. Shangé cut a creature's arm off then sliced the other at the knee, crippling it. She sprinted to help Mijoga just as the door to one of the huts succumbed to the creatures' onslaught. They charged inside and dragged out the struggling occupants. The walaji damu unleashed their shrieks on the hapless villagers, rendering them unconscious. Shangé watched horrified as the creatures lifted the villagers like children onto their shoulders then jumped into the darkness. The other creatures fled as well, hopping after their companions.

Majambere burst from his hut. He ran to Shangé, eyes wide and watering.

"There have never been so many! They came to take us all!"

The others emerged, falling to their knees and lifting their hands to the spirits. Then they saw the violated huts. A wail rose from the village, a lament of pain and loss.

"I failed you," Shangé said.

"No, priestess, you did not," Majambere replied. "If you were not here our village would be no more."

Shangé dropped her head. A dead creature lay between her and Majambere. The others she wounded were gone. It was then she noticed their blood. The thick liquid glowed, giving off a faint bluish light. Shangé grinned.

"I will bring your people back," she said.

"I will go with you," Majambere answered. "I may be able to help."

"No. Stay with your people. They will need your strength and your protection. Mijoga!"

The simba loped to her. Shangé pointed at the blood and Mijoga roared. He sniffed about the body then licked the blood.

"Can you follow them?" she asked.

Mijoga answered with a foreful roar. Together they ran into the night, following the creatures' luminous spoor.

The trail led them to a jagged rip in earth, a crevice crowded with fallen trees and animal carcasses. Shangé had seen the results of earthquakes before; it was how the Land of The Lakes was formed. Another thought began to creep into her head and the reason for her being here became clear. Just as there were spirits in the sky, there were spirits in the earth. And like those above, some were not passive observers.

Mijoga paced. Though he had no knowledge of Shangé's preoccupation it was obvious he sensed something more than a pursuit of some strange creatures. Shangé stroked his mane as she refocused on her immediate task to save the villagers.

"There," she said as she pointed with her sword. A speck of blood glistened on the edge of the crevice. They continued the pursuit, clambering into the darkness of the tear. For a few hours they moved among debris from the surface, but as they journeyed deeper the surroundings transformed into gray stone and stagnant cold. The darkness dispersed, replaced by a weak luminance resembling the walaji damu's blood. It made the trail harder to see, but Shangé's sight eventually adjusted. They were entering another world, a world that existed beyond the touch of Jua and the power of the spirits. Light emitted from everything; the rocks, the stalactites and stalagmites, dousing them with a greenish hue. Glowing insects crawled about the ground and the walls, giving the caverns a sense of movement that unnerved her. They walked through the strange region for hours until the lighted beings dissipated. Shangé hesitated before continuing, waiting for her eyes to adjust. Even with her heightened vision it was still difficult to see ahead. Mijoga expressed his discomfort with a snort and a shake of his head. The walaji damu spoor glowed even brighter, a morbid beacon to its source.

The dark caverns told a different tale that the luminous world. The walls were smooth, the ground rough yet passable. This was no random cave formed by the whims of the spirits; this was a cavern built by skilled hands.

Mijoga roared and shook his head. Shangé looked puzzled until she heard it, a thin piercing sound growing from the back of her mind. She covered her ears to stop the mysterious shriek but it increased with every moment. She fell to her knees, screaming as if her own voice could drown out the sound that stabbed her head like a hot assegai. A deeper darkness settled about her; she was losing consciousness. Something cold gripped her shoulders and a sharp sudden brightness cleared her head for a brief moment. She saw a pale, fanged face then passed out.

* * *

Shangé awoke drenched in pain. The strange emission was gone, replaced by a lingering hum that weighed on her senses. She tried to move; something heavy pressed down on her shoulders, pinning her against a hard surface that pricked her chest. A piercing ache surfaced on the side of her neck, pulsing with the rhythm of her heart.

Images writhed before her. Her eyes slowly responded to the dull light and the forms gained details. Walaji damu danced before a glowing pile of luminous rock, each creature holding a crude stone cup in their hands. A being stood atop the mound draped in an indigo robe sparkling with clear stones reflecting the strange light. It swayed with in time with the others, waving a thick staff over its head.

Shangé twisted her head about. The stolen villagers lay trapped to her right. They knelt before a stone dais, their hands tied behind their backs. A huge stone yoke pressed them down onto the platform. A hollow tube protruded from their necks. Blood dripped from the tube into a stone gourd propped beside the dais. Shangé surmised she was trapped the same way, her blood adding to the feast of the walaji damu.

The blood priest descended the mound and walked towards her. Shange's strength increased with each second, her body healing rapidly. By the time the priest reached her she felt strong and eager to deal with the creatures. She waited; there was a reason for this ceremony beyond what she observed. She would remain still until she discovered it.

The priest took the gourd fill with her blood. He sipped it and his eyes widened. He turned his back to her and spoke in their shrill language, his sounds similar to those that rendered her helpless. The others responded; their movements more vigorous. They assaulted the mound, each one grabbing a portion and raising it high over their heads. The blood priest marched past them and they followed it deeper into the cavern, the light fading fast.

Shangé gritted her teeth and clinched her fists as she pushed her hands apart. The cords binding her wrists held for a moment then snapped like dry straw. She gripped her yoke and grunted, lifting the slab of stone over her shoulders and pitching it forward. It crashed and shattered, shaking the dais on which she lay. She winced as she snatched the blood tube from her neck. Shangé felt about and found her swords propped against the dais. The walaji damu had been confident in her capture and underestimated her abilities. She secured her blades and went to free the others. The villagers had not fared as well as her. They were barely alive, each unconscious and hardly breathing. Shangé was torn between trying to help them and pursuing the cave creatures until a familiar voice sealed her decision.

"I will help them." Shangé turned to see Majambere standing behind her, his face illuminated by a seeing stone dangling from his neck.

"You followed us?" she asked.

Majambere nodded his head. "You travelled too quickly for me to catch up to you. I found you here but there was nothing I could do. I was relieved when the walaji damu left and you freed yourself. Forgive me for my weakness."

"There is nothing to forgive," Shangé assured him. "See to your people. I must go after the walaji damu."

"Wait." Majambere reached into his pouch and extracted another seeing stone.

"You may not need this, but it will help." He looked about curiously. "Where is your simba?"

Fear crept into her head. "I don't know."

Majambere smiled weakly. "I'm sure you will find him, or he will find you."

Shangé put the seeing stone around her neck and went in pursuit of the walaji damu. She ran as fast as the darkness allowed, hoping to quickly close the gap between them. The dimness before her gave way to faint light; she was closing in on the procession. She slowed her pace, staying near enough to follow. She eventually found herself in another cavern, this one more worn and ragged. Though smooth stone covered the ground, the walls showed signs of decay and stalactites dripped from the canopy. The voice of the blood priest rose over the mumbling of the walaji damu as the creatures gathered at the far end of the cavern. Shangé found an outcrop and climb it to see over the throng.

The blood priest stood before a looming grey figure. Its face resembled that of a bat, but its body was more man-like. Long fangs protruded from its wide mouth, gleaming in the light. The priest placed the gourd of Shangé blood before the statue then dropped to his knees. The other fell as well, prostrating before the statue.

But it was no statue. Shangé gasped as a thin tongue extended from the creature's mouth and into the gourd. The organ pulsed and grew thicker as the creature's mouth gaped and its feline-like eyes scanned slowly from side to side.

Shangé slid her swords free. This is what she was sent to do. The walaji damu were not her task, it was the monstrosity awakening before her. She eased off the outcropping and crept toward them.

The creature extended its limbs and the walaji damu began their erratic dance. The blood priest raised his gourd and staff, seeming to urge the creature upward. It stretched to its full height, its massive head breaking the stalactites overhead. The eyes blinked and recognition replaced repose. It struck like a viper, engulfing the blood priest.

The walaji damu froze. The creature snapped up two more before they ran, their high pitch cries no longer stunning Shangé. She was ready for them now, but the hapless beings fleeing around her were no longer her target. She ran towards the blood beast, her swords spread like lethal wings. The creature tossed its head back to swallow its morbid meal. She stopped before it, looking up into the harrowing visage.

The beast struck faster than she anticipated. She barely escaped its bite, stumbling away while swinging down with her sword. The blade grazed its cheek and the creature screeched. It swung its head to the side, slamming it into Shangé and sending her sprawling across the stone. She rolled away from the creature's relentless surges, its head slamming against the stone, the blows having no effect on its ferocity. Shangé finally rolled to her feet and sprang to her left to avoid another lunge. She ducked instinctively, the beast's claws grazing her scalp. She crossed her swords over her head, catching its wrist between the blades then slicing through flesh and bone. The severed paw smacked the stone and the creature screeched. It flailed, the bloody stump spewing black blood in every direction. Shangé stepped and slipped, her head thumped against the stone and she briefly blacked out. The creature was charging her again; she struggled against the throbbing pain in her skull.

The blood creature lunged. Shangé waited then rolled, avoiding the head strike and the grasping arms. She planted her feet then sprang up, both swords pointed above her head. The blades plunged into the beast's throat up to the hilts. It moaned and toppled on to its back, dragging Shangé with it. She found herself standing on its body as it gurgled, its chest sagging inward before falling still.

Shangé tore her swords from its throat. She scrambled off the carcass onto the bloody floor. The walaji damu were gone. Shangé made her way back to the first chamber. Majambere stood beside the dais nursing his villagers. Her head throbbed and her body ached everywhere but she was alive.

She hobbled to the headman.

"Can they walk?"

Majambere shook his head. "Not yet. It will take time for them to regain their strength."

"We don't have time," Shangé warned. "The walaji damu will come back. We must be gone before then."

A strident roar splintered the tense silence. Majambere and the other cowered but Shangé grinned. She knew the sound well, the triumphant call of Mijoga. He strode into their light, his muzzle, mane and claws caked with blood.

"There is no need to hurry now," she told the others. "Our way is clear."

The villagers needed a few more hours to heal then the party set out for the surface. As Shangé said, their way was clear except for the stench of the dead walaji damu littering their course. They emerged from the rift into humid darkness eased by the starlit sky. Shangé did not look up; she feared what she might see. The village came into view and the villagers pace sped in response.

"Come! Come! We are home!" Majambere shouted.

Doors sprang open and the villagers poured out, the night filled with ululations of joy. Shangé and Mijoga stayed back as the villagers hugged, kissed and danced. Majambere broke away from the celebration and prostrated before the two.

"Thank you, priestess," he said. "You have saved us."

Shangé nodded. She finally dared to look into sky. There was nothing there for her, no gleaming patterns, no messages to fill her head.

"Where will you go now?" Majambere asked.

"Where I am sent," Shangé replied.

Majambere studied her for a moment. "I hope you find what you seek."

He stood, bowed, then returned to his people and their celebration.

Shangé watched him for a moment, absently stroking Mijoga's mane.

"I too hope we find what we seek," she whispered. Together they walked into the night, the stars above keeping their secrets to themselves for another day.

MKUU WA SIMBA
(THE LION CHIEF)

Mijoga strode across the open savanna to the nearby waterhole under a clear blue sky, his throat parched and belly empty. As he approached the other animals scattered, all except the kibokos and their mamba companions. The large mammals feared nothing, especially not a lone male simba without a pride. The waterhole was the lair of the reptilian mambas. They would not leave its presence, even in times of drought. None of it matter to Mijoga. A drink of water was all he needed. Once sated he would return to the hunt, hoping to kill something sufficient for him and Shangé.

His simba senses overwhelmed his thought; he sniffed the air before edging closer to the waterhole. The mambas did not swim his way. They had eaten earlier and were not interested in gorging themselves on a lean feline. Mijoga squatted at the water's edge then lapped at the warm water while keeping his eyes on the mambas and kibokos. His thirst satisfied, he set out to find game.

Mijoga rarely thought of his life as a man. He had accepted his fate once his awareness returned. He was grateful for every day he remembered who he was and his love for Shangé, for he knew such days were not guaranteed. There were times he lost himself to the simba. Those days were becoming more frequent. Shangé sensed it, which was why she did not like him separated from her. Her presence helped him hold onto who he was, but it was necessary for him to hunt alone. As special as she was, she was a hindrance when it came to finding food.

Mijoga worked his way to the boundary between the savanna and the forest. Most animals were less attentive when transitioning between habitats, making them easy prey. A scent reached his nose and his ears perked. It was not the scent of game; it was man scent, the smell of fear. Moments later the sound of rapid footfalls and breaking branches reached him. He backed away, curious about the scene unravelling to his senses. Minutes later a man burst from the forest. A group of robed men with chains and spears followed. The spectacle was a familiar one to Mijoga and anger filled his chest then escaped in a load roar. The robed men halted, turning in his direction. Their eyes gorged with fear when they saw the massive simba charging toward them, mouth wide and fangs bared. They fled back into the woods, cursing and yelling. No potential slave was worth their lives.

Mijoga waited at the forest's edge to see if the slavers would return. Once he knew they had no intentions of doing so, he looked for the man they pursued. Mijoga found him on his knees, gasping for air. Mijoga approached him, knowing that his presence would frighten the man. He was

right. The man turned to face him then screamed. He prostrated before Mijoga, his desperation clear.

"Great simba," the man said. "You have spared me
from the slavers. Please spare me from your jaws!"

The man looked into Mijoga's eyes and Mijoga was tak-
en aback. If his feline countenance could have shown
shock, it would have. He knew this man. Mijoga opened
his mouth and a roar emerged. For a moment he'd forgotten his current state and tried to speak to the man he once
knew as Ita. Ita cowered, holding his arms over his head.
Mijoga backed away, not knowing what to do. Ita was far
from their village, and if he was being chased by slavers he
was not alone. Had the slavers raided their village, or had
they captured Ita alone? Mijoga had to find out.

He shook his head then jogged away from Ita. A nearby
acacia offered shade, so he sauntered to it then plopped
down. He lay his head on his forelimbs then closed his
eyes, feigning sleep. Through his half-closed eyelids he
watched Ita stand. He looked about then ran toward the
woods. Mijoga waited until Ita was no longer visible before
standing and trotting toward the forest. A scent caught his
attention and the simba inside him arose, triggered by his
increasing hunger. His mouth watered. An antelope herd
had come to the waterhole, oblivious to his presence and
taking their chances with the lurking mambas. His body
veered in their direction, the simba asserting his instincts.
But Mijoga would not be swayed. He forced himself to
roar, startling the herd and sending it into flight. The simba
subsided, allowing Mijoga to continue his pursuit of Ita.

Ita's odor was strong, but Mijoga kept his distance. He followed the man's trail for hours until Ita halted just before dusk. His odor was usurped by the smells of others. Mijoga surmised there was a camp nearby, most likely the one Ita escaped. He crept through the foliage until he could see Ita crouching, most likely waiting until dark to approach. Mijoga worked his way around then moved closer to the camp. What he saw stunned him into blind anger.

His people were chained together, forced to sit side by side. The slavers served them from small bowls with just enough food to keep them alive and moving. A few strides away the slavers feasted, exchanging words and laughs as his people languished. The anger burned from his chest throughout his body. Mijoga felt himself transforming as his anger became uncontrollable. When he stood, he was no longer Mijoga the simba. He was Mijoga the man.

Mijoga hurried to find Ita. The man was still where he last saw him, staring at the camp from his hiding place.

"Ita," Mijoga said.

Ita spun toward him, his fists raised.

"You have nothing to fear from me, old friend. I am here to help you."

Ita's expression went from anger to shock. He lowered his hands, his mouth agape.

"Mkuu Mijoga?" he said. "Is it really you, or have I lost my mind?"

"It's me, Ita," Mijoga said. "Though for how long I do not know."

Ita rushed to him as quietly as he could then hugged him tight.

"We thought you were dead!" he said. "We all saw when the Ancestors came and took you. We were sure we would never see you again. And now you stand before me. If it were not for the situation of our people, I would be crying for joy."

Mijoga pushed Ita away then pulled him down to a crouch.

"I am happy to see you, Ita, but we must deal with the circumstances at hand. How did this happen?"

Ita scowled. "It's Nyaga's fault. He became mkuu after your death . . . I mean your disappearance. He said he wanted to make the village richer. He said we would take our extra harvest to Sofala where we would trade it for jewels and other valuables then sell those to the other villages. We would take what we earned to cultivate more fields. The people believed his words. It was his greed and theirs that brought us to this day."

"That does not explain why our people are held captive," Mijoga said.

"The Sofalans were not interested in our grain," Ita continued. "They were interested in us. Our bodies were worth more to the Omanis than anything we could grow or hunt. When our traders reached the city, the Omanis returned with them. They filled Nyaga's head with their lies and he sent them back with more grain and ivory. When they returned, they brought more men and shackles and chains.

"How many were captured?" Mijoga asked.

"Everyone," Ita replied. "They took many in the first raid, including Nyaga. Those who remained fled to the forests, but it did not matter. When the Omanis came the second time, they found us. Nyaga was leading them."

Ita spat as he said Nyaga's name.

"We must free them," Mijoga said.

"How?" Ita asked. "I have been thinking about this ever since I escaped. I am encouraged that you are here because I know the Ancestors are with us. But still, we are only two. They are many, and they are armed."

"We are not alone," Mijoga said. "We will have help soon."

At least that was what Mijoga hoped. Shangé's tasks were guided by the Elders, and as far as he knew this had nothing to do with her. This was his challenge he would have to face alone.

"We will wait until nightfall," Mijoga said. "We will take the guards first then claim their weapons. You will free our people and lead them away."

"What will you do?" Ita asked.

"I will make sure no one follows you," Mijoga said.

Ita was silent for a moment before speaking.

"It is not a good plan," Ita said. "I am weak, as is our people. I have no doubt in your skills, mkuu, for I have seen you fight many times. But not even you can hold back so many."

"It is a chance," Mijoga replied. "You must choose between slavery or freedom."

Ita nodded. They waited in the bush as the sun took its time descending below the horizon. Ita shared what little food he had with Mijoga. It did not quell his hunger nor silence the simba inside him, but it would have to do. As soon as darkness swallowed the savanna Mijoga made his way toward the camp. His senses were just as keen in his human form as they were as a simba, which made it easy to spot the guards on the camp's perimeter. He slowed his pace so Ita could keep up.

Together they made their way to the south side of the camp. The smell of the captives overwhelmed him. Their dismal conditions saddened and angered Mijoga. The guard sat before them, trying his best to stay awake. An empty gourd of palm wine was his nemisis.

Mijoga struck swiftly. He sprinted from the woods, covering the guard's mouth with his left hand as he locked his right arm around his neck. He dragged the man's body away; the guard was dead before he reached the woods. Mijoga searched the man and found the keys to the chains. He gave them to Ita.

"You know what to do. Once you free everyone run as fast and far as you can."

Ita nodded then went to his people. He shushed them with his finger against his lips, then freed them one by one. Once he'd released them all, he gestured for them to follow him into the bush.

Mijoga donned the clothes and weapons of the guard then walked into the camp. He approached the closest guard, his head lowered to hide his face.

"Azizi! What are you doing here? You're supposed to be . . ."

Mijoga stabbed the man in the throat. He jerked the sword free and let the man fall to the ground. He proceeded to the center of the camp occupied by the Omani leaders' tent. Mijoga took a burning stick from the nearby fire, tossed it on the tent then waited.

The Omanis yelled as they fled the tent. Mijoga waited at the flap, striking them down as they appeared. He was about to strike the last man when his instincts warned him of danger. He crouched and the spear meant for his back flew over his head. The others had come as he had hoped. What he didn't anticipate was that there would be so many. The fighters were draped in traditional Swahili and Omani garb, brandishing curved swords and broadleaf spears. One man was dressed in the clothes of a villager, a short sword in his hand.

"Nyaga," Mijoga said.

Nyaga snarled, then his eyes went wide.

"Mijoga?"

Mijoga realized he could not defeat so many, at least as he was. He dropped his weapons, closed his eyes then released the simba. His transformation caught his adversaries by surpised. They stepped back, giving Mijoga the time he needed.

Mijoga smiled inside at Nyaga's stunned face as he pounced. He sank his teeth in the man's throat then tore them free. Nyaga was dead before his back touched the dirt. The others had fled after seeing Mijoga transform into the simba. Mijoga turned to flee.

"Why are you running?" he heard a voice say. "He is just a beast, and a beast can be killed."

Mijoga spun about as the warriors returned. The man leading them caused a twinge of fear from the simba. Mijoga searched his memory and discovered why; the man was a Samburu, a simba killer.

"Surround it!" the man ordered.

The warriors did as told, forming an iron-fanged ring around Mijoga.

"Attack!"

Mijoga twisted from side to side, the warriors prodding him with their spears. They were too timid to come close enough for a deep wound, but that was not their task. The Samburu waited for the moment that Mijoga's strength faltered then he would move in for the kill. Mijoga had no fear or regret; the longer they toyed with him, the more time his people had to escape.

A cry came from behind the men before him; seconds later an Omani fell from the darkness, landing before his paws. The sound of clashing metal filled his ears and the warriors fell away one by one. As the last man collapsed, their attacker stepping into the light of the burning tent.

"Mijoga," Shangé said. "What is going on?"

The warriors behind him lost heart and scattered into the woods. Mijoga walked up to Shangé, pressing his head against her hip. She knelt then hugged him.

"The Elders told me you were in danger. Why are here attacking these men?"

Mijoga trotted to the woods and Shangé followed. It took them an hour to catch up with the fleeing villagers. One of the people in the rear glanced back and saw them, her face slacked, and her eyebrows rose.

"Simba!" she shouted.

The people cried out then tried to run.

"Wait!" Another voiced called out. It was Ita.

Mijoga waited until the man appeared. He stared at Mijoga then his eyes went to Shangé.

"There is nothing to fear," he said to the others

Ita came to them. He prostrated before Shangé.

"Honored Spirit," he said.

"Who are you?" Shangé asked.

"I am Ita. I was . . . I am Mkuu Mijoga's friend."

Shangé turned to Mijoga, a shocked look on her face.

"These are your people?"

Mijoga answered with a rumble. Shangé turned her attention back to the man.

"How do you know this is Mijoga?"

"He revealed himself to me," Ita replied.

"The Elders had a hand in this," Shangé said to Mijoga. "They sent you to save your people, and you did."

Ita stood. He moved close to Mijoga.

"Everyone, come," he said. "I promise you there is nothing to fear."

Ita touched Mijoga's mane then looked to Shangé.

"You are the spirit he loves," he said.

"Yes," Shangé replied.

"It is fitting," Ita said. "The Ancestors could not bring themselves to destroy him. It is good that they didn't. Without him we would be lost."

The others came closer as Ita turned to face them.

"This is Mkuu Mijoga," he said. "He serves the Ancestors now. It is he who first saved me, then you."

The villagers prostrated before Mijoga. Sadness overwhelmed him and he roared. The people raised their heads and smiled.

"We are happy to see Mijoga again," Ita said. "Take care of him, Honored Spirit, as I know he will take care of you.'

"I will," Shangé replied. "Watch over your people, Ita. You are their mkuu now. So says Mijoga."

Ita bowed again then backed away until he reached the villagers.

"Let's go home," he said.

The villagers parted to let Ita through then followed him into the bush.

"Come Mijoga," Shangé said. "The Elders summon us. Your people are in good hands."

Shangé headed north through the camp. Mijoga looked into the darkness where his people had once stood. He roared, then followed Shangé to their new destination.

WALEZI
(THE GUARDIANS)

Shangé and Mijoga ran toward sounds of struggle. Two weeks ago, the Spirits contacted them, sending them on this journey. Their information was vague, but their commands were clear. Mijoga was the first to hear the struggle, roaring then plunging into the bush. Shangé followed, never doubting his instinct. The sounds of clashing metal reached her ears moments later, joined with the grunts and curses of men.

"Watch its claws!"

"Be careful! We don't want to harm it!"

"The woman is useless. Kill her!"

The last statement fueled their limbs. A shrill cry unlike any she'd ever heard drowned out the men's voices and caused Shangé to hesitate. Whatever these men fought was not natural to her world.

Mijoga strode into the clearing before her. Shangé followed soon afterwards and was stunned by the sight that greeted them. Eight men with swords, spears, hooks and nets surrounded a woman armed with a spear sitting upon the back of a creature Shangé could barely remember, one which all, even the spirits, thought long dead. The beast stood on two legs, striking out at the men with its stunted clawed forelimbs. It snapped at them with its large head, baring its fangs. The woman stabbed at the men with her spear, attempting to keep them at bay. Though they fought valiantly, it was obvious both were exhausted. It was only a matter of time before the men overwhelmed them.

Mijoga roared, breaking the men's focus. Two of them turned to the simba and Shangé, dropped their weapons then fled into the bush. One man fell, his neck pierced by the spear of the woman riding the beast. The others backed away on their guard.

"This doesn't concern you!" one of the men shouted as he glared at Shangé.

"That's not your decision to make," Shangé replied.

The men attacked.

Mijoga met the first man with teeth and claws, taking him down immediately and silencing his cries by ripping out his throat. The others ignored their cohort, pouncing on Shangé with fervor. She sidestepped them both, cutting one man across the back with her swords as she ran toward the woman and her beast. Mijoga took down the other man as he tried to pursue her. The remaining men looked at her and their potential prize then fled into the bush.

Shangé sheathed her swords as she approached the woman and her strange mount. Mijoga charged by her toward the pair, a roar escaping his open maw.

"Mijoga, no!" Shangé said.

The beast lowered his head, emitting a sound that resembled that of the great birds. Its rider pressed her legs into the beast's sides, patting it on its neck. The creature backed away, its eyes locked on Mijoga. Mijoga let out another roar then returned to Shangé.

The woman dismounted then ambled toward Shangé. Yellow leather armor protected her chest and lower body, her mid-section exposed. Broad beautiful earrings hung from her lobes, her headdress snug on her bald head. She halted a few feet from Shangé and Mijoga then prostrated before them both. To Shangé's surprise, her creature did the same.

"Thank you, guardian," she said. "I was not sure you would come."

It took Shangé a few moments to decipher her words. The language she spoke was old, one Shangé had not heard in centuries. It was thought among the Spirits that the First Ones were gone. Apparently, it was not so.

"Please rise, daughter," Shangé said. "I am not worthy of your reverence."

The woman stood, a warm smile on her youthful face.

"It is good the Spirits still remember us," she said. "We thought you had forgotten. I am Luam. This is my bond, Wubet."

Shangé approached the woman, her arm extended.

"I am Shangé," she said. "This is Mijoga."

Luam face became solemn. "He is your lover."

Shangé lowered her hand. "How did you know?"

"I can see his ka." she said.

Luam walked by Shangé to Mijoga. He nuzzled her face as she embraced him.

"He aches for you," Luam said. "He struggles with the simba he has become."

Luam stood, her eyes on Shangé. "You must release him soon or you will lose him to the simba."

"I know," Shangé said. She was impressed by Luam's perception, but there were other things she needed to know.

"Luam, why were these men trying to kill you?"

"They weren't trying to kill me," she answered. "They wished to take Wubet alive . . . if they could."

"Where are your people?"

Luam's response was guarded. "Far from here."

"Why are you so far from home?"

"We came looking for one that belongs to us," Luam replied. "When we found her, these men had claimed her life."

Luam gestured to her right. Shangé and Mijoga walked in the direction and found the body of the creature. Parts had been harvested by the hunters.

"She is at peace now," Luam said. "At least she will not suffer more."

"We should bury her," Shangé said.

Luam shook her head. "No. Let her body feed those that thrive around her."

Shangé's curiosity was sparked by this mysterious woman and her companion.

"I ask you again, Luam. Where do your people live?"

Luam smiled.

"Come. I will show you."

* * *

Sadiki and Gamada watched the women and their beasts fade into the distance. As soon as they disappeared Gamada gathered his weapons. The stocky man did a quick inspection then signaled Sadiki.

"Let's go," he said.

"No," Sadiki replied.

Gamada glared at the lanky Swahili then shrugged.

"Allah be with you," he said, then started walking away.

"Wait!" Sadiki called out. "Don't you realize where they're going?"

"I don't know, and I don't care," Gamada said. "I'm alive and I plan on staying that way."

Sadiki held up the bag that contained parts of the lizard-like beast they had slain.

"That woman and her beast are probably from the same place the mamba came from."

The creature was not a mamba, but Sadiki had no other name for it.

"That means there are more of them."

"And more of her, too," Gamada retorted. "And with the other woman and that simba, that's too much for me."

"We don't have to fight them. All we need to do is follow them."

Gamada stopped then turned.

"And then what?"

"We report back to Bwana Jabili and let him know. I'm sure he can gather enough hunters to overwhelm whatever we encounter. He would raise an army for what this bounty would earn him . . . and us."

Gamada rubbed his chin. "I don't know . . ."

Sadiki approached him.

"We won't be in danger. We will stay far enough behind them that we won't be noticed. We'll mark our path, so we'll know how to return. But I can't do this without you. You're the tracker."

Gamada smirked. "I'll do it, but I'll want half your take."

Sadiki's eyes widened. "Half? You greedy nyani!"

"I wish you well," Gamada said then walked away.

"Okay, half!" Sadiki agreed.

Gamada grinned as he sat down his pack.

"Let's get some rest then."

"Rest? We have to follow them now!"

"No, we don't," Gamada said. "I'm the tracker, remember?" It's dry season. We have time. So unpack and get some rest, partner."

Sadiki frowned as he followed Gamada's suggestion.

The blood red sun emerged over the horizon, spilling it hue over the verdant savanna. Shangé was stirred awake by a rough tongue on her cheek. She grinned as she reached up and pushed Mijoga's head away.

"Good morning," she said.

She sat up then stretched. A beautiful voice accompanied by bird-like whistles reached her ears, raising her spirits higher. Luam sat before a fire concocting their morning meal while Wubet loomed over her. It was they who made the music, singing together as they did everyday of their two-week journey. They seemed to have an endless repertoire, each song as lovely and captivating as the next. Mijoga sat next to her as they listened. They both were disappointed as the song ended when Luam stood to bring them their meal. Her smile was as warm as her songs.

"I hope you rested well," she said as she extended the bowls of stew to Shangé and Mijoga. Shangé's bowl was filled with wild vegetables gathered from the surrounding flora; Mijoga's bowl was similar with the exception of chunks of meat as was his need in his simba form. The food was delicious. Luam seemed to have an infinite knowledge of their surroundings, no matter where their journey took them.

"Thank you," Shangé said. "Luam, are we close to your home?"

"Very close," Luam replied. She pointed to the distant mountains.

"There," she said. "We have another day's walk."

Shangé studied the mountains and was puzzled. These were not the verdant mounts that existed in the south. They were hard gray columns of jagged stone capped with snow.

"It must be a harsh life," Shangé said.

"No, it is paradise," Luam replied. "You will see."

They resumed their trek after the meal. They walked in silence, the animals of the savanna keeping a distance from the odd quartet. Shangé felt a peace she had not experienced in quite some time. Being in the presence of Luam and Wubet seemed to steady her. Why, she did not know. But she would savor the feeling until she determined the real meaning why she was sent to aid them. The encounter with the hunters was serious, but from what she now knew of Luam, the situation would have ended in her favor. She listened for guidance from those above, but they remained silent. This would be a quest she would have to decipher on her own.

On the second day they neared the mountains. The peaks had long since disappeared, too high for them to see from their vantage point. Shangé worried as they came closer, for she did not see any trails or paths into the rugged heights.

"I do not see where we are going," she said.

Luam smiled. "Of course, you don't."

"Are sure this is the right way?"

"It is our home," she replied. "I am very sure."

They finally reached the mountain. Shangé continued to be confused. There was no path leading into the upper peaks and no sign of any dwellings. Luam and Wubet walked parallel to the base, humming another tune. Suddenly they disappeared. Shangé ran to where she last saw them, Mijoga close behind. She was about call out when a hand reached out then pulled her into darkness.

"Luam?" she asked.

"Hold my hand," Luam said. "Grab Mijoga's mane. We will lead you."

"But it is too dark to see."

"One does not need sight when the path is in your heart."

Shangé grasped Luam's hand then clutched Mijoga's mane. The woman pulled her forward and she followed, trusting her guidance. The way became darker, a void so dense Shangé could feel it on her skin. She hesitated.

"We cannot stop here," Luam said. "If we do, we'll be lost."

Shangé felt the ground giving way. She gave in to Luam's pull and continued following her. The ground became firm again; a trickle of light appeared before them. The darkness finally faded, the ragged cliff walls coming into view. The path widened and brightness flooded the narrow path. Luam let go of her hand.

"We are safe now," she said. "We are home."

Luam sang a new melody and Wubet joined her. Though Shangé didn't understand their secret language, she could feel the joy in their words. Their song was answered, a chorus of voices rising from the distance. They emerged from the crevasse and were greeted by a lush forest filled with vegetation. Shangé had to reach deep into her memory to recall such a place. Mijoga halted, his simba instincts overruling his human sensibilities. He sniffed the air as he gazed about, his actions relaying his nervousness.

A host emerged from the forest, men and women mounted on beasts similar to Wubet, all singing the same song. They formed a ring around Shangé, Mijoga, Luam and Wubet, raising and lowering their spears in unison. Luam stopped singing.

"They celebrate our return and welcome you," she said. "We will follow them, and you will meet the elders. They will be happy to see you."

The singers formed a line, walking in rhythm through the woods until their city came into view. Tall wooden structures capped by grass roofs arose from the trees, separated by wide dirt-packed avenues lined by fruit trees and other edible flora. The people emptied their homes to observe the impromptu procession, adding their voices. Shangé had never witnessed anything so welcoming since falling. She wondered if this was her reward; had the Spirits finally deemed her worthy of freedom? Her thoughts were dampened as she looked at Mijoga. Her lover turned simba swayed his head from side to side, his keen eyes studying all those they passed. If the Spirits had forgiven her, Mijoga would be in his human form, or at least she hoped he would be.

The homes diminished until they reached the city center. A huge baobab tree stood before them, its dense canopy providing shade for the benches below. Elderly women and men sat at the seats, yet they rose when they saw the procession. They sang as well, their eyes bright as they met Shangé's.

The followers dispersed, leaving Shangé, Mijoga, Luam and Wubet in the Elders' presence. They approached the seated council, who prostrated before Shangé

"Please, do not honor me this way," Shangé said.

A tall woman with gray braided hair stood then approached, hobbling with a sturdy wooden cane crowned with the image of a nyani.

"We are honored to have you, priestess," she said.

"I am no priestess," Shangé replied.

"You fell from the sky," the woman replied. "For this reason only, you deserve our honor."

"Her name is Shangé," Luam said. "And this is her lover, Mijoga."

The old woman's eyebrows rose as she gazed upon Mijoga.

"A man should know better than to desire a spirit," the old woman said. "A spirit should know better as well."

Shangé frowned. "You sound like my mother."

"Wisdom often comes from the same sources," the old woman said. "But we will not dwell on past actions. You and your companion are welcomed among us. May the Spirits Above grant you your blessing."

Shangé watched the others gather around them, their beasts walking side by side with them. Maybe this was the place the spirits were guiding her to all along. The people of this land lived in perfect harmony with their beasts, much in the same way she shared her life with Mijoga. If there were ever to be a reprieve from those who judged her, it would most likely happen in this land. Mijoga nudged her, a soft growl coming from his mouth.

"You sense it too?" she asked.

Mijoga responded by licking her hand.

"So we agree. I think we are home."

* * *

Sadiki and Gamada trudged through the crowded streets of Mombasa in search of the Swahili merchant district. Sadiki stopped person after person, hoping to locate the home of the merchant who financed their excursion into the bush for the strange creatures. Gamada's expression conveyed his displeasure with his partner. Coupling that with the fact that he was a man who disdained the city, he was not in a very good mood. He stopped in the middle of the street then folded his arms across his chest. Sadiki was almost out of view of the hunter before he realized Gamada was no longer following him. He spun about then stomped back to the hunter.

"Why are you just standing here?" he asked.

"I should never have let you talk me into this," Gamada replied. "You tricked me to bring you back here. You can't talk the merchant into paying us. You don't even know who he is!"

Sadiki raised his hands in defeat.

"I don't, but that doesn't matter."

Gamada shoved Sadiki so hard the man almost fell.

"Hey!" Sadiki shouted. He was regaining his balance when Gamada shoved him again. Sadiki fell onto his back. Before he could stand Gamada stood over him, his hunting knife in his hand.

"I should slit you open from your jewels to your throat!"

A crowd gathered around the men, some of them shouting for Gamada to put his knife away, others urging him to make good on his threat.

"Do it and you'll never get paid," Sadiki said.

"Paid by who?"

"Why do you think I'm asking everyone? Bwana Jabali is a man who has ears everywhere. If we can't find him, he will find us."

As Sadiki finished his words Gamada felt a sharp prick on his neck. He looked sideways to see the point of a kashkara pressed against his skin. The man holding the sword was dressed in traditional Swahili garb, his white turban contrasting with his black skin.

"Who are you?" the man asked. "And why do you spout Bwana Jabali's name from your foul mouths?"

Gamada gestured with his blade at Sadiki.

"Ask him."

The man stared at Sadiki, awaiting an explanation.

"I am one of the men bwana Jabili sent to find the walking nyokas. Gamada, the hunter, was one of our trackers."

"Get up," the man ordered. Sadiki scrambled to his feet then dusted off his clothes.

"Both of you follow me."

Gamada and Sadiki trailed the man as he weaved through the crowded market to the merchant district.

"See, I told you it would work," Sadiki said.

"Don't speak to me," Gamada replied. "Once I get my pay, I'm gone from this place."

"You can't leave!" Sadiki said. "You are the only one that knows the way. I told you I'd give you half of my pay!"

"That's not enough. I'll tell whomever you hire to take my place how to get there. I'm done with the lot of you."

Bwana Jabali's house stood out from the others in the merchant district because of its size and beauty. Even Gamada was impressed. Jabili's man opened the metal gate to the courtyard and the two followed him inside. As they reached the center of the courtyard the man turned to them.

"Wait here," he ordered.

The man entered the house. Moments later he emerged, followed by two sentries and a servant carrying a large chair. Behind the servant was Bwana Jabili, a stout man wearing rich clothing and a bright red turban.

The servant placed the chair before Gamada and Sadiki. Bwana Jabili sat as the guards flanked him. The third guard remained by behind the duo.

"I sent ten men to bring me a walking Nyoka," Jabali said. "Where are the others?"

"They are dead," Sadiki said. "The nyoka we encountered was controlled by a warrior. Another warrior commanding a large simba attacked us as well. Only Gamada and I were able to escape with our lives . . . and this."

Sadiki gave Jabili the bag. The merchant opened it and a smile came to his face.

"I knew the stories were true!" Jabili said. "This is most fortunate."

The merchant turned his attention to Gamada.

"You know the way?"

"Yes," Gamada said. "But I will not take you there. You can find another hunter and I will share my knowledge with him."

Jabili frowned. "That is not acceptable. Husani?"

The guard standing behind them snatched his kashkara free then cut off Sadiki's head. Gamada watched in horror as Sadiki's head hit the ground, his body falling beside it. His hand went instinctively to his knife, but he knew it was in vain. The other guards stepped toward him, their swords drawn.

"Put your jambiya away, hunter," Jabili said. "You don't stand a chance. Besides, I have no intention of killing you. You know the way. Sadiki was expendable, as were the others."

Gamada looked at Sadiki's remains. He did not like the man, but he didn't deserve to die like this. Still, Gamada had no intentions of sacrificing himself for Sadiki's honor.

"In their defense, we did not expect to be attacked," he said.

"It doesn't matter," Jabili replied. "I'll put together another expedition and you will lead them. I will pay you one fourth of what we bring back. That should make it worth your while."

"I'd much rather be paid than killed," Gamada said.

Jabili smiled. "I thought so. Husani will take you to an inn where you can rest. You will depart in two weeks. Do not fail me, Gamada."

Gamada swallowed hard.

"I won't, Bwana Jabili."

*　*　*

Shangé strolled through the flower field, Mijoga by her side. The low bellows of the long-necked beasts grazing not far from them were soothing to her ears despite their enormous size. It had taken Mijoga some time to get used to the creatures, but he eventually settled down. The meat eaters still made them both nervous, but the People assured them that they were no threat. The People had trained them to feast from the rivers and lakes instead of on their brethren. If that had not been accomplished neither plant eaters nor flesh eaters would exist, and neither would the People.

Shangé knew she and Mijoga should leave the valley, but she could not. Never had she felt so at peace since being sentenced to a human shell. Though Mijoga was still trapped in his simba form, the bond between them was closer than she'd ever experienced. If she could not have him as a man, this existence was the best they could choose. He did not struggle with his animal side; there was a balance that seemed to be strengthened by this wonderful place.

Their walk took them to the lake. Mijoga waded into the waters and immediately returned with a plump fish. He entered three more times, returning with a fish. Shangé gathered wood then built a small fire. She foraged for edible plants then prepared a meal for them both. They ate slowly, as they did everything in this wondrous land. If Mijoga never returned to his mortal form, she would be content with him in this place.

They ate untill they were full then slept by the shimmering water. A soft touch woke her. She opened her eyes to Luam's friendly face.

"Hello, Shangé. "Mama wishes to speak with you."

Shangé sat up then rubbed her eyes.

"Where is she?"

A bright smile filled Luam's face.

"Communion."

Shangé straightened. Communion was the People's sacred ground, a place where they honored their ancestors, both human and otherwise. To be invited meant the People had accepted her and Mijoga into their clan. For some reason, this pleased Shangé.

"We will go immediately."

"There is no hurry," Luam said. "Mama is patient. Wubet and I are going. You can come with us."

"We would love to," Shangé said.

She shook Mijoga awake. He responded with a loud roar that expressed his annoyance.

"Forgive me," Shangé said. "But we have been invited to Communion."

Mijoga understood the significance of her words. His eyebrows rose and it seemed as though he smiled.

Shangé turned to Luam.

"We are ready."

The four walked along the edge of the lake until they reached the fields near the foothills. Luam and Wubet sang as always, lulling Shangé into a sense of peace. They followed a narrow trail through the fields which led to the forests covering the foothills of the looming mountains. The air became colder yet tolerable as they entered the trees. After a few more moments of walking, they reached a steep rift that descended into darkness. Luam turned to her.

"Mama waits for you," she said.

"Thank you," Shangé replied. "Come Mijoga."

Mijoga roared then stepped away. He gazed into the darkness with uncertainty in his eyes.

"There's nothing to fear," Luam assured them. "There is only peace where Mama waits."

Shangé knelt beside Mijoga then hugged him.

"Come Mijoga. I sense no danger here."

She stood, her fingers tangled in Mijoga's mane. She tugged at him gently and he followed her down the steep slope into the dense woods. They treaded through dimness, yet Shangé sensed their destination. The forest was void of sound except their footfalls and their breathing. Shangé pressed closer Mijoga as the woods darkened. She saw nothing, but she sensed everything. A powerful spirit waited for them, something beyond anything she'd experienced in a long time.

"Mama," she said.

Shangé let go of Mijoga and ran. Mijoga roared then pursued her through the blackness, his way barred by the trees. Shangé was aware of his distress, but she could not help him. She needed to know what was this power drawing her through the foliage. She emerged into a wide clearing of grass and wildflowers. Mama stood in the center of the field, wearing in a black dress that fell to her bare feet. There was a look of serenity on her face, but Shangé knew that was not her expression. A spirit from above sat on her head, one that Shangé called Mama. Mijoga came to her side then immediately laid on the ground, his head lowered.

"You know I must go alone," Shangé said. "She still does not approve of you."

Mijoga shook his mane.

Shangé sauntered to her mother then knelt before her.

"I am honored to see you," she said.

"As am I," mama replied. "The people you are among are precious to me. There was a time that I walked the earth with them."

Shangé raised her head, her eyes wide. Although she knew many of the celestial pantheon were once human, she didn't know her mama was among them. It explained her leniency when Shangé was given her punishment.

"Their lives will soon be threatened," her mother continued. "Many of them will not survive."

Coldness swept through Shangé. That anyone would wish to harm these people angered her.

"So, our encountering Luam wasn't by chance," she said.

"Nothing you do is," mama replied.

Her mama approached and placed her hand on Shangé's cheek. Shangé had never touched her mother in physical form, yet the contact was as familiar as it was in the heavens. Tears came to her eyes.

"I'm so sorry," she said.

"There is no need to apologize. Your emotions are you own. The others do not understand. They are not like us."

Mama reached down and pulled Shangé to her feet.

"We are always watching. What you do here will mean much to us all."

Shangé looked at mama with resolve.

"I will not fail you," she said.

"You could never fail me. Now go. Spend what time you have with Mijoga."

"What?"

Shangé jerked her head about. Mijoga stood in his human form, a wide grin on hi face.

"Hurry," mama said. "Your time with him is short."

"Thank you, mama!"

Shangé ran to Mijoga, who waited with open arms. Together they tumbled to the ground, their laughter filling the open field until more amorous matters occupied their time.

* * *

Gamada did not like what he was seeing. For two weeks he had been a 'guest' of Jabili, although prisoner would have been a more appropriate word. During that time men arrived every day, the type of men Gamada wouldn't have looked at, let alone spoke to. They came from cities as far away as Mogadishu and as close as Mombasa. No matter what their origin, they all possessed the same demeanor. This was not going to be a hunting expedition. All these men were killers. This was going to be an attack.

Though the men worried the hunter, they did not frighten him. Gamada was not a killer, but because he was a hunter he knew how to kill. He was not a skilled fighter, but he was an effective one. The person causing him worry arrived two days ago. Her presence disturbed him like an animal sensing danger. Gamada had a good idea what she was, but he attempted to keep such thoughts out of his mind. Dangerous feelings brought dangerous times, and he was already in too deep.

"Hunter!"

Gamada winced when Jabili called his name. He turned slowly and his mood fell deeper when he spotted the woman standing beside the merchant.

"Yes, bwana?" he responded.

"Come closer."

Gamada trudged to the duo, his head bowed.

"This is Atiena," Jabili said. "She will be in charge of your expedition. You will give her the same respect that you give me. Is that clear?"

Gamada nodded. "Yes, bwana."

"Lift your head so I can see your eyes," Atiena said.

Gamada lifted his head, his eyes turned away.

"Look at me!" she shouted.

Gamada's head jerked to her as if she had grabbed it with her hands. Their eyes met and he was swallowed into a haze of blurred images. The imageries slowed until he was reliving the journey that led them to the discovery of the giant lizards. A sharp pain struck his head and his vision cleared. The woman continued to stare at him, a smirk on her face.

"What did you see?" Jabili asked.

"Not much," she replied. "He protects his secrets well. I didn't see enough not to need his help. He must come with us."

Gamada wasn't sure, but he thought his life had just been spared. Both Jabali and Atiena seemed disappointed.

"You will lead the expedition to the place where you encountered the mambas," Jabali said. "Once Aiena confirms your information, you will be free to go."

Gamada knew that was a lie. He would be killed as soon as he was no longer needed.

"Will I be paid?" he asked.

"Of course," Jabili replied. "I am a man of my word."

"Thank you, bwana," he said.

"You may go," Atiena said. "We leave at sunrise."

Gamada did not sleep that night. He spent the time trying to devise a way to save his life. He could take them the wrong way, but sooner or later Atiena would discover his ruse and have him killed. Again, he thought of taking the chance of escaping, but the camp surrounding Jabali's home was well guarded. Gamada was a brave man in the bush, but among humans he was unsure. He would have to wait until he was in the countryside before planning his flight. To try in the city was fruitless.

The morning finally arrived, the call for prayer drifting on the winds from the nearby mosque. Gamada was the first to rise, checking his weapons and supplies. Jabili had provided well for the expedition but Gamada stashed away his own provisions to make sure he would not be hindered when he attemptd his escape. It wasn't much but if he ran out, he could live off the land as long as he needed. The only decision to make was where he would go. Wherever it was, it had to be away from any Swahili trade routes.

The camp awoke around him. He meandered through the tents, lending a hand when needed. Though he was totally against this safari, he had to appear otherwise. He felt eyes upon him and turned his head to see Atiena staring, a frown on her hard face. She did not trust him, and she had every reason not to. But she was resigned to working with him at least until they reached their destination. Gamada slid his hand into his pocket and touched the bag of gris-gris he purchased days ago in the Mombasa market. He hoped it would protect him from Atiena's nyama, but he would only know when the time came. He reached into his kpinga pouch, fingering the leather wrapped handles. If the gris-gris didn't work, maybe the knives would.

The party departed at noon. They marched through the city, Atiena and Gamada leaning the warriors and porters to the boats taking them across the lagoon separating Mombasa from the mainland. When they reached the mainland, they followed a well-worn trail into the bush until dusk.

"We will camp here," Gamada said to Atiena.

"Why?" she asked.

"The trail will be challenging from this point.

Atiena tilted her head as she frowned.

"Stop here!" she shouted, her voice carrying far beyond that of a normal person. Gamada felt a chill run down his back. He closed his eyes to stabilize his emotions then began walking into the bush.

"Where are you going?" Atiena asked.

"Hunting," Gamada replied. "This is a good area for springbok. I may be able to bring one down to add to our meal."

"I'm coming with you," Atiena said.

Gamada shook his head. "No. You'll make too much noise."

Atiena grinned. "You'll be surprised how quiet I can be. Deadly quiet."

Gamada understood the meaning of her words. She was not going to let him out of her sight until he was no longer useful.

"Come then. We only have a few hours of daylight remaining."

Atiena followed him into the bush. She was as quiet as she promised. Gamada didn't know if it was because of skill or nyama. For the time being it didn't matter. The hunt went well; he killed two springboks. Atiena helped dress the animals and also carried a good portion of the meat. If she wasn't a threat to his life, she would be a good hunting companion. The men were grateful to have fresh bush meat to add to their meal. Gamada smoked that which they didn't eat then stored it away, sneaking a healthy portion into his personal stash.

The routine remained the same for the following days. Atiena was a complex issue; although he knew she was keeping an eye on him, her company was pleasant. Gamada suspected she was trying to lull him into trusting her but he knew better.

On the tenth day out of Mombasa they neared the location where the deadly encounter with the woman and the walking mamba occurred. Gamada slowed the pace, his nervousness growing by the moment. Atiena joined him, a frown on her face.

"What is it, Gamada," she asked.

"I'm trying to determine where the fight happened," he said. "It has been some time."

Atiena laughed. "You can remember the trails of tembos, the best place to hunt game, but you cannot remember where you fought the walking mambas? You're lying, Gamada."

"You can't read my mind," Gamada snapped.

"No, I can't. But I can read your body. You're tense; your eyes show your fear. By looking at you I believe we are close, very close."

Atiena trotted ahead of him, reaching into a leather pouch on her belt. She stood still, pulled her hand from her pouch then chanted in a tongue he did not understand. She tossed the powder into the air. Instead of drifting on the wind it swirled over her head like a miniature tempest. Gamada walked backwards as Atiena concentrated on the swirling powder. His eyes widened as the dust thinned into a thread then began undulating in the direction where the bloody incident took place. Gamada needed to see no more. He spun and ran as fast as he could for the bush. Atiena knew the way; he had become expendable.

"Kill him!" Atiena shouted.

Gamada flattened on the ground. Arrows flew over him; he rolled then clambered to his feet as more arrows pierced the ground where he had once laid. He sprinted for a clump of thorn bushes, moving from side to side to avoid being struck by the arrows. The arrows ceased as Gamada ran beyond bow range; he glanced behind and saw three of the mercenaries pursuing him. He slowed his pace, knowing that sooner or later he would have to fight them and he wanted enough energy remaining to have at least a chance to survive. The warriors ran faster as they neared, one of them letting out a whoop as he drew his sword. Gamada took one more glance, making sure he remembered their positions as he eased a throwing knife from his pouch. After a few more steps he spun about and threw his knife. The weapon struck his target in the face; the man fell screaming and clutching at its hilt. Gamada took out his sword and dagger, holding both low as he charged. The second warrior, sensing an easy kill, grinned as Gamada attacked him unguarded. As he stabbed at Gamada's gut the hunter pivoted to his right, slashing the man's throat with his sword then stabbing him in the kidney with his dagger. He kept spinning until he faced the third warrior. The man stood ready, a sword in each hand. Gamada would not be able to fool this one. He would have to fight without trickery.

The warrior attacked, thrusting and swinging both swords. Gamada scrambled back, staying out of range. He snatched another throwing knife from his bag and threw it; the warrior batted it away with his sword. Gamada tried to move in on the warrior but the man recovered quickly. Gamada winced as the blade cut across his chest. He spun with the momentum of the blow then fell onto his stomach. The warrior moved in for the kill. Gamada rolled onto his back and the blade almost missed. He cried out as the sword pierced his side at the same time as his sword sank into the warrior's throat. The dying warrior continued to fall forward, Gamada's blade pushing out the back of his neck. Gamada twisted away, letting the man fall by his side. He lay on the ground, his torso bleeding, hoping the others assumed he was dead. He also hoped Atiena was too distracted to make certain. After two hours he realized he was right on both accounts.

Gamada sat up then inspected his wound. It was not as bad as he imagined, but he needed to treat it quickly before it became infected. He checked his surroundings one more time before standing then staggering toward a clump of acacias and shrubs. When he reached the cover, he sat and tended his wound with a few healing items he had packed with his supplies. Once the wound was treated and covered, he pulled out the strips of springbok he smoked earlier and ate. As he chewed, he contemplated his next move. He was free of Jabili and the witch; he could go on his way and never see neither of them again. But why was hesitating? It only took him a moment to answer; he was angry. Atiena tried to kill him for no other reason than not wanting him to know the way to the lair of the walking mambas. He assumed the same fate awaited the men that were with her. Once she claimed what she and Jabili desired they would be disposed of. He decided that night Atiena did not deserve to find the walking mambas. He packed his supplies then set out after the group. They had a few days head start on him, but Gamada was travelling alone. He would catch up with them, then he would contemplate his next move. Whatever it was, it would end with Atiena's death. Of that, he was certain.

* * *

Atiena hummed as she followed the thin smoke trail leading her to the location where the walking mamba encounter took place. In truth, she did not need its guidance; the nyama emitted from the mambas still lingered. It was a powerful, intoxicating sensation, like following the sun at noon. Jabili was right to contact her; the talisman harvested from the walking mambas would be more powerful than any she encountered. She wondered if there were more, and if so, how many more. Whatever that number might be, Atiena knew this treasure was not meant for Jabili. That fool would sell it to the highest bidders after keeping a substantial amount for his own power and protection. None of the others realized what type of force they dealt with. They did not deserve it, and Atiena would make sure they never received it.

Night came, forcing them to set up camp. Atiena waited in her tent to be served, feeling anxious. They were so close. She rushed through her meal then waited patiently as the warriors settled then fell to sleep. As soon as the last man slumbered Atiena was on her feet and running through the camp, her destination the place of the walking mamba battle.

She was well into the night when the sensation almost overwhelmed her. She stopped to reorient herself, blinded by the glaring spirituality radiating ahead. It took a moment to channel the power, her eyesight clearing with each second. Finding her foundation again, she proceeded to the site. She saw her destination, the area glowing as if laminated by light. Atiena knew that wasn't the case; this was spiritual aura, something that only she and others like her could see.

Atiena walked to the center of the light then sat. The power enveloped her, pulling images from her mind. She saw her childhood, growing as a girl under the tutelage of her mother and grandmother as they taught her the wisdom and skills of their craft. She felt the sorrow of her grandmother's passing, then her mother, both entrusting their nyama to her as they transitioned into the spirit world. She was too young to fight the pull of the darker magic. Not that she minded. It had always been there, lurking at the edge of her consciousness, waiting for its opportunity to offer itself. The moment came as her mother drew her last breath.

The impressions shifted from the past to the present. She saw a land surrounded by massive mountains filled with flora that no one had seen in thousands of seasons. Then she saw them, massive majestic animals, creatures that no human had ever seen alive. They roamed the vast grasslands and forests of this hidden valley, predator and prey coexisting without fear. And then she spied them, humans that walked with these beasts, sharing a strange benevolent connection. She was focusing on the bond between these animals and humans when two spirits intruded on her focus, overwhelming the others with their spiritual presence. Atiena eyebrows moved closer as she focused on the beings, finally getting a glimpse of their forms. One was a simba, yet its spirit was that of a man. Then there was the woman, who was like nothing Atiena experienced. She appeared as a human, but her spirit revealed her as something much more. Atiena tried to look closer but the woman's nyama was too strong. The woman turned her head toward Atiena. A surprised look gripped the woman's face and the images were scoured from Atiena's mind. She fell onto her back, gasping for air. These were no mere animals they were hunting. These animals and their human caretakers possessed more power than she had imagined.

She stood, her legs unsteady. She staggered back to the camp, a grim frown on her face. Whoever these people were, they would not give up their treasures easily. There would be a battle, and many would die. She would have to make sure enough of her people survived to claim the bounty of the hidden valley. She would not fail.

* * *

Shangé woke with a start, the image of the woman still in her mind. Her name was Atiena, and she had come to claim the creatures of the valley. The anger she felt cleared her grogginess and pulled her to her feet. Mijoga still slept; Shangé started to wake him but thought better of it. Instead, she went in search of Mama. When she arrived at Communion, Mama sat with her eyes open, a welcoming smile on her face.

"Mama," Shangé began.

"I know," Mama replied. "We must prepare."

"Mijoga and I can handle them," Shangé said. "You and the others will be safe here."

"No, you cannot," Mama replied. "Atiena is as intelligent as she is powerful. She will prepare her warriors for the battle to come. You will put up a grand struggle, but the two of you alone would fail."

"That is not possible," Shangé replied. "I will not let that happen."

"Search your heart, Shangé. You know this to be true."

Shangé closed her eyes, clearing away the emotions that would block her vision. She saw the battle without the others and the outcome was clear. When she opened her eyes, they were filled with tears.

"I'm sorry," she said.

Mama nodded. "Our passing is inevitable. None were meant to live forever. Our only hope was to transition peacefully. Those who will go with you understand what they must do. They will fight the others; you and Mijoga will take care of Atiena, if you can."

Shangé nodded. "Your valley will be safe. I promise you."

"You cannot make such promises," Mama replied. "Now go. They will be here soon."

Shangé sprinted away. She found Mijoga still sleeping. Kneeling before him, she dug her fingers into his mane then shook his head.

"Mijoga, wake up."

Mijoga grunted then opened his eyes. He pushed his head against her gently then stood.

"Others are coming to attack the valley. We must defend it."

Mijoga's eyes narrowed before he let out a defiant roar. Shangé smiled.

"Yes. We will fight them. Come; let us find Luam and Wubet."

They hurried back to the main village. The streets were busy, humans and creatures going about their daily business. Shangé and Mijoga found Luam and Wubet at the city market. They were singing as always, but this time there was an audience enjoying their talents. Shangé hesitated, knowing that her news would their lives for the worse. So, she listened for a time despite knowing that time was of the essence. Mijoga nudged her. She looked into his eyes and saw his sadness as well.

"I know," she said. "It's time."

She broke the audience ring and approached. Luam stopped singing and shared a smile with her.

"What is it, sister?" she asked.

"I must speak with you," Shangé replied.

Luam's smile faded. She reached back and touched Wubet's snout.

"Come Wubet."

They followed Shangé away from the market, stopping at the first open area.

"The hunters are coming again," Shangé said. "They are bringing many warriors and a powerful sorcerer. We must assemble outside the valley to confront them."

Luam took on a solemn look which Wubet answered with a low croon. Sadness welled in Shangé's chest upon hearing the sound.

"As you command, Shangé," Luam answered.

A sound came from her mouth that was similar to Wubet's moan and carried throughout the village. It was answered by dozens of voices, then shared by everyone. Tears came to Shangé's eyes. Luam looked at her then smiled.

"Lead us," she said.

Shangé and Mijoga led Luam and Wubet from the village. As they made their way to the grassland others joined them, accompanied by their familiars. Shangé looked about and was fascinated by the variety of companions. This was truly a haven for them, a last homeland for beasts and people who had once claimed this land as their own. A loud croon came from the forests as the largest of the beasts emerged into the open, their human companions riding on their backs with their weapons in their hands. They gathered to protect their home, knowing that many of them would die. An old feeling overcame her, the love she felt for these creatures she was once responsible for. With it came the shame of falling in love with one and denying the others the protection that was meant for all. She glanced at Mijoga then patted his mane. Mijoga looked up at her, sharing his emotion through feline eyes. Shangé focused on the journey ahead, hoping she could stop the oncoming threat before it destroyed them all.

* * *

A huge bonfire illuminated the night, the unnatural flames surrounded by nervous warriors. They had gathered against their will, forced to take part in a ceremony that they would rather not witness. But for them to refuse meant risking death, so they circled the fire and silently prayed for their ka.

Atiena sat cross-legged before the flames, chanting as she ground a concoction of herbs and remnants of the slayed beast on the seasoned surface of her mixinig stone. She took special care in measuring out the amounts, for this elixir would make the difference in the coming battle. As skilled as the warriors were that accompanied her, they were no match for the horde they would soon face. The potion she prepared would even the odds.

Atiena completed the powdery mix. She opened the gourd of water beside her then poured the powder inside. She shook the gourd, chanting the names of the various spirits that assisted her magic, hoping they would hear her. As he ended the mantra, she threw the gourd into the fire. After a few minutes she retrieved the container with her staff then let it cool. Atiena scanned the warriors, making eye contact with each one of them.

"Come forward," she said.

The warriors came with their cups in their hands. Atiena picked up the gourd and pulled the ceramic plug free.

"Drink it quickly," she said, "then return to your tents. It will make you sleep. When you awaken, you will be reborn."

The first man approached her, beads, his cup trembling as sweat beads formed on his forehead.

"Don't be afraid," Atiena whispered to him. "I will not harm you, if only because I need you."

She poured a small portion of the elixir in his cup and he drank it immediately. The bitter brew caused him to frown for a moment before a pleasant expression took over his face.

"Go to your tent," she said.

The man nodded then hurried away. The others were less anxious than the first man, seeing that he did not fall dead in front of them. Most of them did as she told them, going to their tents before the potion took effect. Others did not heed her words. They collapsed where they stood, falling asleep on the ground or wherever they were when the potion triggered. She wandered the camp after all the concoction had been administered, making sure every warrior slept. She was against her now. There would be a battle, and they would be victorious. The potion would keep the warriors at their peak until the fight was over and the walking mamba parts collected. A simple word from her lips and the elixir would become a poison and kill them all. When she returned to Mombasa, only one person alive would know the location of the valley.

* * *

Gamada observed the activity around the bonfire from his hiding place. The ancestors had seen fit to grant him the eyesight of the great birds, so he witnessed everything in detail. He saw the warriors put to sleep by the witch's brew then watched her inspect the camp before going into her own tent. Gamada waited another hour before he began his trek to the camp. It was a foolish thing to do; the witch had almost killed him before and would not make the same mistake twice. He wasn't brave enough to try to kill her in her tent, but he had to know what the witch had given the others. He crept into the camp, his sword in his trembling hand. His first destination was the bonfire. He hoped the witch left remnants of the elixer in the gourd. She had not.

Gamada then went to check the warriors who had fallen asleep in the open because of the potion. He finally found one man who still had some of the potion in his cup. Gamada stuck the tip of his finger into the liquid then touched it on his tongue. His eyes went wide as he tasted it, then he ran from the camp making no effort to hide his departure. He sprinted until he was out of sight then he snatched the water bag from his waist and rinsed his mouth over and over again. After his bag was empty, he ran to the nearest water hole and began rinsing his mouth again. He was no sorcerer, but he was familiar with some of the ingredients the witch used in her potion. The warriors who drank it were doomed to death and didn't even know it. Gamada's anger boiled to the surface and he considered charging into the camp and trying to kill the witch, but he knew he would fail. He would bide his time and wait for the right moment.

* * *

The sun rose as Shangé and Mijoga led the others from the secret passage onto the savanna. The warriors and their sorcerer had not arrived, so they had time to develop a strategy. Luam and Wubet walked with them as they crossed the grasses, the land eerily empty of the normally abundant fauna. It was as if the animals knew what was about to take place. In contrast the guardians seemed calm. Luam and Wubet sang and the others joined in. The tune soothed Shangé's emotions. She knew many of them would die, but she also knew they would join their ancestors knowing they had done what they could to protect their people.

The horizon became ragged with the outline of approaching people. Shangé felt the strong presence of the sorcerer and she removed her swords from their sheaths. Luam glanced at her and her song changed. The others tensed as they sang in response.

"This is not your doing," Luam said to Shangé as if reading her mind. "The Spirits sent us to you for this moment. Because of you, many of us will survive. For this, we are grateful."

"I hope I can save all of you," Shangé replied.

"That is not possible," Luam said.

Shangé focused on the presence of the sorcerer. She lingered behind the warriors, expecting them to take the brunt of the attack while she waited to strike once Shangé and the others were weak. Shangé had a different plan.

As they neared Shangé felt another sensation. It pulsed among the warriors approaching them.

"Luam," she said. "Be careful. The warriors have been infused with nyama. They will be more difficult to defeat."

"I feel it," Luam replied. "But it does not change our resolve. We will make a way for you to the sorcerer. The sooner you kill her, the better for us all."

Luam let out a shrill whistle. The others responded and together they ran toward the approaching warriors.

"Luam! Wait!" Shangé shouted, but it was too late. Luam had not given her time to share her plan. The people's defenders crossed the distance with amazing speed. By the time Shangé and Mijoga was halfway to them the fighting had begun. The Walezi were outnumbered, but they made up the disadvantage with their ferocity and their size. The warriors surrounded them, their enhanced abilities aiding them but not giving them the easy victory they sought. Shangé wanted to stop and help the Walezi, but she knew the best way she could do so was to find and defeat the sorcerer. She sprinted up the path the Walezi cut for her, avoiding the warriors as she sought the sorcerer.

The woman was not hard to find. She sat on the ground, her legs crossed and hands folded in her lap. She stood as Shangé and Mijoga came closer. A grin came to her face before she thrusted her hand toward them. A wall of force struck them both. Shangé held her ground; Mijogo roared as he was lifted up then slammed into the dirt. A painful howl escaped him as he hit the ground. Shangé wanted to help him, but she could not. She had to defeat this woman.

The sorcerer sent another blast toward her. Shangé sliced with her swords, dissipating it. The sorcerer strode toward Shangé as she opened her hands. Shafts of light formed in her palms, coalescing into swords. The women clashed, the shock wave from their blows tumbling some of the warriors and Walezis. The sorcerer matched Shangé every move with power Shangé had never experienced from a human. She pressed her attack but the sorcerer held her ground.

Something blurred by her, the sorcerer dodging it at the last minute. It was Mijoga, recovered from the initial at- tack. He was still wounded yet he struck with all the energy he could muster. The sorcerer battled both of them, seem- ing to grow stronger with each moment. Shangé began to doubt if she could defeat her. Her eyes narrowed as she pressed on. She would not let the Walezi and their people die.

* * *

Gamada used every bit of his skill as he crept closer to the fighting women. They seemed evenly matched as they fought. He considered using his bow, but he didn't want to chance missing his target. He would have to get close with his knife so he could be sure. It was very possible he would die even if he was able to kill Atiena, but he would take that risk.

Gamada hesitated when the simba appeared. There was something different about it; the way it moved was unusual. He watched the fight for a moment, then began his slow advance again. He was finally within reach. He came to his feet, the knife gripped firmly in his hand.

"Atiena!" he shouted.

The witch turned her head and rage filled her face.

"You!"

Gamada plunged toward Atiena. His knife almost found its mark before he was struck by something hard and sharp in his stomach. He rose into the air then slammed hard onto the ground. Gamada stared into the sky, the sun dimming with his fading eyesight, a grin coming to his face. This had not turned out as he planned.

* * *

Shangé didn't know what distracted the sorcerer but she took advantage of it. She slashed the woman across her back, the blow spinning her around. Their eyes met as Shangé drove her sword into the woman's stomach. The sorcerer looked at her with no expression as she dropped her swords and grasped Shangé's blade. She grunted as she slowly pulled the blade from her body. Shangé did not wait for her to complete what should have been impossible. She swung her free blade, cutting off the woman's head. Shangé let go of the blade and the woman's headless body fell to the ground, her hands still clutching Shangé other blade. It was then she saw the reason for the sorcerer's distraction. A man lay on his back, bleeding from his stomach. Shangé wanted to go to him, but she had to aid the Walezi. She extracted her blade from the sorcerer's body then ran to help. Her heart dropped at the sight before her. Though they had decimated the warriors, most of the walezi were dead. Luam, Wubet, and three other pairs continued to battle, their songs of defiance rising over the clashing of blades. Shangé plowed into the warriors from the rear, her whirling blades making quick work of them. Moments later all the warriors lay dead or dying.

The walezi singing ceased. Shangé fell to her knees, weighed down by sadness. Luam and Wubet walked up to her, Luam smiling despite the loss surrounding them.

"We have done our duty," Luam said. "It is all we can do."

"But your loss is so great," Shangé answered.

"Yet we still survive," Luam replied.

Shangé stood. "I wish I could have done more."

"You have done enough," Luam said.

Her eyes focused beyond Shangé. She patted Wubet's neck and they went to the dying man who had distracted the sorcerer. Luam climbed from Wubet's back then knelt beside the man.

"Who are you?" she asked.

Gamada's eyes opened then widened.

"Gamada," he said.

"You will come with us."

She lifted Gamada from the ground as if he was a child. Wubet knelt and she climbed onto his back with the man.

Shangé approached them, Mijoga limping by her side.

"Are you sure you can trust him?"

"His soul is good," Luam said. "And we have suffered losses. He will bond with one of the old ones. I am sure of it."

Shangé felt a warm sensation inside, a sign that her work was done.

"I wish you well, Luam," she said. "I hope your people will never be threatened again."

Luam shared a wise smile with Shangé.

"One day we will no longer be," she said. "But we will perish knowing that we did our best to protect our people. Farewell, Shangé and Mijoga. I hope one day the Spirits grant you the peace you deserve.

Luam sang and Wubet joined her. They merged with their cohorts then sauntered toward the mountain and their hidden home. Shangé and Mijoga stayed until they could no longer hear their songs. Once silence befell them, they turned away from the mountain and followed the Spirits calling them to a new destination.

ABASA'S PROMISE

Shangé awoke in confusion. She sat up, grasping about for her weapons and searching frantically for Mijoga. It took her a few moments to realize that she'd been asleep. She sat still, breathing deeply to calm herself. Sleep was a new state for her, something she had yet to become accustomed to. As a spirit the condition did not exist. For months after her exile she did not sleep, her conscious mocking her former state. But gradually the demands of her body would not be denied. Sleep usually caught her off guard. She often awoke on rugged surfaces in awkward positions which caused her to ache for hours or days afterwards.

She rubbed her eyes then looked about. Expecting to see Mijoga lounging nearby as he always did, she jumped when she saw the back of a nude man stretched out beside her. How he came so close without her knowing she couldn't understand. It was especially puzzling that Mijoga did not warn her.

"Mijoga!" she shouted, not caring if she woke the interloper. The man stirred and her heart raced.

"Mijoga?" she said again.

"What?" the man replied.

Shangé grabbed the man's arm then rolled him over. She gasped when she saw his face, a face that she had held in her memory for years, hoping she would see once again. Tears filled her eyes as she smiled with joy.

"Mijoga! Mijoga!" she sang as she shook her lover from the grip of sleep.

He knocked her hands away. "Shangé, what . . ."

It took Mijoga a moment to realize what had occurred. His eyes widened then he inspected his body. He gazed at his hands, his arms, his manhood, his legs and his feet. Shangé followed his motions until their eyes met and he shared with her the wonderful smile that drew her down from the heavens and into his arms, the arms she ached to be held by.

They leapt at each other, hugging and kissing almost violently before falling into lovemaking just as spirited. When they were done, they held each other tight, afraid to let go of what they both desired for so long.

"You are forgiven," Mijoga said, his voice as resonant as she remembered.

"Yes, I am," Shangé replied.

"And they have let you stay with me," he said.

Shangé kissed him. "Yes, they have."

Mijoga looked skyward, "I guess I will stop cursing them."

He held her tightly and pain bit into her back. Shangé pushed away as Mijoga let her go.

"What is this?" He looked at his hands in horror. They transformed before his eyes, back into the paws they had once been.

"No, no!" Shangé shouted.

Mijoga fell to the ground in spasms as his body reverted. Tan fur usurped his skin, his hair extending into a tawny mane. The last to revert was his face, his eyes filled with hate then finally resigned to the fate that had been forced upon him. The pain was still in his eyes after he resumed his feline form. He looked at the sky then loosed a mournful roar before running into the bush.

"Mijoga!" Shangé reached out to him but could not follow. She collapsed where she stood then curled up on the grass, her body racked with sobs.

"It is a sad fate you are forced to live."

The strange voice forced her to her feet, swords in hand. She looked at a tall, muscular man wrapped in leather and leopard skin, his look on his patterned face reflecting her emotions.

"Is this how our gods reward us for love? By punishment?" he scowled. "Such beings do not deserve our praise."

"Who are you?" Shangé demanded.

"I am Abasa," he replied.

Shangé thought for a moment then her hands tightened on her swords. "Are you responsible for what just happened?"

Abasa looked away. "I am."

Shangé raised her swords then Abasa raised his hands.

"I did not do what I did to offend you. I did it to show that those above are not the only ones that can grant you reprieve."

"How do you know of us?" Shangé asked.

"I am a shaman," Abasa replied. "The spirits talk to me. Your story is an especially sad one. I sought you out to help you. With the proper items I can lift your punishment. You and Mijoga can live a life of man and woman, with a home and children. I can grant all of this to you, but first you must do something for me."

Shangé continued to hold her swords at guard. For years she roamed the land as servant to those she once shared the sky, doing their bidding as penance for a grievous violation; loving what she was chosen to protect. Now a stranger claiming to have powers beyond those she served was promising to free her of this burden. She knew the Spirits should have something to say about this if it was possible. But they had been silent.

"You wish me to believe you can break that which was forged by those much stronger than you?"

Abasa nodded. "Did you not see what I did with what little I have?"

"An illusion, nothing more," Shangé said.

"If it was so you would know," Abasa replied. "Wouldn't you?"

She was silent. What she had seen was true nyama, the strongest she'd witnessed from mortals.

"What is it that you seek?" she finally asked.

"You are not the only being that has fallen from the sky," Abasa said. "There is one that descended long ago, a being that possessed power far beyond any we can imagine, even those that you serve."

"That is impossible," Shangé said. "If such a being exist, I would know of it. I would feel its presence."

"Yes, you would, if it was alive," Abasa said.

"Now I know you lie," Shangé replied. "For such a being death would not exist."

"It does, yet it doesn't," Abasa said. "There is no reason to explain this to you any further if you do not agree to help me. There are others that have the ability. I will not waste any more time with you if you have doubts. The transformation of your lover should have been proof enough."

Mijoga returned to her as if summoned by Abasa's last words. He roared at the shaman then stood by Shangé's side, pressing his mane against her hip.

"What must we do?" Shangé asked.

Abasa smiled. "Come to my encampment. There are others you should meet. They suffer as you do."

Others that endure like her? Shangé was skeptical.

"We will come, but I make no guarantees," she finally said.

"Good," Abasa replied. "Follow me."

Mijoga and Shangé followed Abasa across the rolling grasses and through herds of grazing animals. His encampment emerged over the horizon after a few hours. It was an elaborate site, one resembling that of a travelling person of power. An entourage came from the camp to meet them, its excited members gathering around Abasa and showering him with all manners of praise. After a few minutes of adulation, they broke away from the sonchai and descended on Shangé and Mijoga. They showed no fear of Mijoga, speaking to him as if they knew he could understand and digging their hands into his mane to massage his scalp, something Shangé did almost every night. Mijoga made no threatening moves toward any of them, contributing to her awkward feelings.

A woman appeared before Shangé, a young umber-skinned beauty with styled knots of hair covering her head. She wore a simple green kanga that fitted her narrow body.

"Are you the star goddess?" she asked. Shangé was surprised by the question.

"I am no goddess," she replied. "But I did once dwell among the stars."

The woman smiled. "I am Aisha. Baba Abasa has long searched for you. You are the key to opening eternity."

Shangé was disturbed by her words. She was about to confront Abasa when the woman grabbed her arm and pulled her away.

"Come with me," she said. "We have prepared a feast for you and the others. You must get to know them before we go on our safari."

The woman led Shangé to the center of the encampment. A large fire blazed surrounded by smaller cooking fires where the meals were being prepared. Drummers ringed the outside of the clearing; they began playing as soon as they saw Shangé and her escort. Dancers appeared from the tents, moving their supple bodies in time with the vigorous rhythm. Shangé found herself enchanted by the cadence, her steps falling in synch. But it was the food that captured her the most. Being a creature that did not often desire such earthly demands she had never developed a fondness for it, especially that made of flesh. But the aromas filling her senses caused her to desire food like she'd never before. By the time she took her place among the others she was famished.

It took her a moment to realize Mijoga was not with her. Shangé looked about, panic growing inside. She was just about to shout his name when Aisha appeared before her with a bowel of fruit.

"Do not worry about your simba friend," she said. "He is being well taken care of. Would you like some fruit?"

Shangé eyed the woman suspiciously. There was no reason she should distrust her and the others, but their joy seemed to be unnatural. She took the fruit then bit into it. It was as delicious as it looked. She chewed slowly, trying to detect some unnatural ingredient but tasted nothing.

"Abasa said you would enjoy this," Aisha said.

"How would he know?" Shangé asked.

"Because Abasa knows everything!"

She motioned with her head toward the others.

"Come, you must meet your companions!"

Aisha took her arm then pulled her to the dining table. As she neared the details of the others became clear. A man sat at the end of the table. He was broadly built with muscled shoulders. It was his head that stood out, resembling that of a faru, a long-curved horn where his nose would be. He was being fed by a slim woman with elongated arms covered with feathers. They both looked at Shangé briefly then continued their meal. There was another person at the table. She sat still, staring at the bowl before her. She slapped it away and stood. The woman glared at Shangé before stalking away into the darkness, her footfalls e heavy. It was then Shangé noticed the woman was made of stone.

"Sad, isn't it?" Aisha said as they reached her seat. "Each one of them has been cheated by the spirits. They have great powers, yet they are deformed by their gifts. Abasa will fix them, as he will your friend Mijoga."

Shangé said nothing. A fragrant bowl of stew was brought to her that tasted as good as it smelled. She looked at the others; they stared at her but still did not speak. She shrugged. Conversation was not necessary for her, but she had learned during her journeys that humans have a need to communicate in order to build emotional bonds. Her senses told her they were not yet ready to accept her, so she remained quiet.

Aisha waited for her to finish her meal. As soon as she was done the woman picked up the bowl and handed it to a servant.

"Come," she said. "I will take you to your sleeping tent."

Shangé followed the woman, her fatigue increasing with each step. By the time she reached the tent she could barely keep her eyes open.

"What have you done to me?" she asked, her voice slurred.

"Do not worry," Aisha replied. "Abasa wanted to make sure you slept so you will be ready for our journey. The others will be helpful, but your powers are the most precious. We need you ready."

Shangé stumbled and Aisha caught her. The woman was strong for her size. She guided Shangé to the bed then placed her head on the headrest.

"Mi . . . Mijoga," Shangé managed to say.

"He is coming," Aisha assured her.

With those words Shangé fell asleep.

* * *

"Shangé."

The resonant familiar voice stirred her. Shangé lifted her head from the headrest then looked to her right. Mijoga the man lay beside her, a mischievous smile on his face. Shangé wanted to fall into his arms but she did not.

"How long?" she asked.

Mijoga's smile faded. "I don't know. Abasa told me the process would not be permanent. I can only be a man at night. During the day I must take the simba form."

"He toys with us," Shangé said.

133

"I know, but what can we do? When you help him claim what he seeks my transformation will be permanent. We will be free of them. We can live a normal life."

"It won't be that easy, Mijoga," she said.

"Most likely not, but we have faced much together. We will face this, too."

Shangé touched Mijoga's cheek and he grasped her hand.

"The nights are ours," he said. "Let's make the best of them."

They made love until their bodies were utterly drained. Shangé slept like never before, finally embracing the human necessity. When she awoke the sun was full in the sky and Mijoga was gone. Standing over her bed was Aisha.

"You are finally awake," she said. "Abasa told me not to disturb your rest, but be close by when you did."

Shangé rubbed her eyes.

"Where is Mijoga?" she asked.

"He has gone to hunt," Aisha replied.

"He couldn't have. He never goes hunting without me."

"He is changing," Abasa said

The sorcerer entered the tent, his eyes lingering on Shangé's nude body. She was not normally bothered by anyone seeing her in such a way, but Abasa's stare disturbed her. She quickly donned her clothes and secured her weapons. When done she glared at Abasa.

"What does she mean by Mijoga is changing?" she asked.

"In order for him to make a complete transformation his mind must be separated from that of the simba he possesses," Abasa explained. "During the day he will be a true simba in every way. He does not remember you or his life as a man. But as the sun sets, he transforms into his true self. Unlike the simba, he remembers his love for you and the curse you both suffer, which makes it more important that we leave immediately. The sooner we arrive at our destination, the sooner you and your lover can be one as for as long as you live."

"Abasa, everyone is ready," Aisha said.

"Good," he replied. "Our journey begins."

Shangé followed Abasa and Aisha out of the hut. The others were leaving the camp, the porters loaded with baggage marching single file. The feathered woman and the faru man walked before the caravan; the Stone woman trailed behind. Shangé decided she would walk with the Stone woman.

"Be careful," Abasa warned. "Harisajiwe can be very volatile."

Shangé did not answer. She had been the patron of humans for millennia. She knew them well.

She walked to the woman then fell in beside her, matching her ponderous gait. They said nothing as they walked, Harisajiwe glancing at her from time to time. When they took their first rest they sat together under a small tree. Shangé ate what they served; the stone woman took no food. Instead, she stared at Shangé as she ate.

"I've forgotten what food tastes like," Harisajiwe said.

"I never knew," Shangé replied.

"How could you not know?"

"Where I am from there was no need to eat. This frame requires it, and Abasa's food seems quite appealing."

"There is much that is appealing about Abasa, but the sooner I'm rid of him the better. No such thing as an honest sorcerer."

"Is a sorcerer the reason you are as you are?"

"Of course, it is!" Harisajiwe shouted. "How else could this have happened?"

"You could have angered the spirits, as I did."

The stone woman seemed to calm down.

"When this is over, we both can have our revenge."

"I don't seek revenge," Shangé said. "I only wish to live my life as I choose."

"Then I will seek it for both of us," Harisajiwe said.

The bird woman and the faru-headed man approached them. Harisajiwe stood then stalked away, visible disturbed by their presence.

"She flitters away again," the woman said in a voice that matched her form. The faru man shorted then plopped on the ground, shaking it. The woman sat beside him then stroked his head.

"We saw her talking to you and thought you'd made a breakthrough," the woman said. "She only speaks to Abasa and when she does, she is always angry."

"She has her reasons," Shangé said.

"I am Kiden," the woman said. "This is my brother Kajok. He is normally very talkative, but the sorcerer's punishment has rendered him speechless. I was once the quiet one, but now I must speak for the both of us."

"What did you do to draw the wrath of the sorcerer?" Shangé asked.

"Dufu," Kiden said. "His name is Dufu. He came to our valley in a storm then claimed himself our ruler. Our warriors tried to defeat him, but he was too strong. He proclaimed that half of our harvest belonged to him, as did our cattle and our goats. Then he chose those from among us to live with him as his servants. While we starved, they flourished."

Kajok grunted and nodded his head. Shangé felt his anger as a hot wind against her skin.

"Our parents fell ill, as did our siblings. When they died it was up to Karok and I to take care of the others. We decided we would sneak into Dufu's compound and steal enough food to leave the valley and find somewhere else to live. But Dufu's servants captured us and took us to him. We waited for him to kill us; instead, he turned us into monsters then forced us to watch our sisters and brothers starve to death. Afterwards he wrapped us in a storm that swept us so far from our village we could not find our way back even if we wished. It was during our wanderings that we found Abasa."

"And he has promised to change you back," Shangé said.

"Yes."

"And you believe him?

"Abasa is not like the others. He found us performing in a village to earn cowries to eat. He approached us and told us who he was and what he could to for us. We didn't believe him, of course, until he changed us."

"Like he did Mijoga," Shangé whispered.

"What did you say?" Kiden asked.

"Nothing. Please continue."

"There's nothing else to tell, really. We've been with him ever since, waiting for the day that we can make our transformation complete. And now that day is near. I'm so excited!"

Shangé smiled but she could not share Kiden's joy. She desired for Mijoga to have his former frame more than anything, but she was suspicious of Abasa's claims.

The group resumed their journey. They traveled though the savannah into the high pasture, eventually crossing the low hills to descend into a rocky valley. The second day was spent crossing a turbulent river swollen by recent rains. The task was so tiring they spent the next day at rest, Shangé anticipating the night so she could spend time with Mijoga. During the entire journey Shangé had seen Abasa only from a distance. The sorcerer seemed constantly preoccupied, spending his time giving orders to his servants and having intense conversations with Aisha. However, two days after crossing the river, the sorcerer found his way to Shange's side.

"Tomorrow we will reach the temple," he said. "Tomorrow will be the end of your suffering."

"How can you be so sure?" Shangé asked. "I have spent most of my life among the Spirits. I know what true power feels like. Although you are powerful, I don't think you are strong enough to transform all of us. Such a task would take more than you possess."

"You are correct," Abasa admitted. "On my own I could not help any of you. As a matter of fact, I doubt if could fulfill my promise to you, let alone the others."

"So, you have misled us all," she said.

"No," Abasa answered. "The temple we seek contains all the nyama needed to keep my promise and much more."

"I know of no talisman or gris-gris so powerful."

"What rests in the temple is neither. It is infinitely more potent."

Shange's skepticism was clear on her face.

"So the temple contains the one we spoke of when we first encountered you."

"Yes."

"What is it then?" she asked.

"It is the soul of a god," Abasa replied.

"That is impossible," Shangé said. "Like I said before, gods do not die."

"True, but they transform. You are not the only celestial being seduced by the ways of man. Centuries ago, this being was seduced to Earth. It existed among humans for centuries, not realizing its power was slowly diminishing. By the time it realized it, it was too late. It did not have the strength to return it its own world. It built a temple and encased itself inside, hoping to replenish its power and one day return to the Sky."

"And you intend to prevent it."

"You must ask yourself what you want most," Abasa said. "Either you wish to be reunited permanently with your lover or you put the well-being of a spirit you owe nothing to over your own. I will honor whatever you decide, but know that if you decide not to, you condemn Harisajiwe, Kiden and Kajok as well."

"You cannot place that guilt upon me," she said. "I did not promise them a transformation."

"No, you didn't. I did. But your decision will prevent my actions."

Shangé marched away from Abasa filled with anger. She did not believe in violating graves, yet if she chose not to, she would not receive the transition she wanted, nor would the others. Although she could endure her consequences, she did not know how the others would fare.

"They are not your responsibility anymore," she said to herself. "You owe them nothing."

The words were easy to say; the emotions were more difficult. When Mijoga came to visit her that night there was no lovemaking. Instead, they lay entwined in each other's arms as she told Mijoga of her dilemma. The former chief took on a thoughtful look as he considered her words. When he finally looked into her eyes, Shangé saw his pain.

"I want nothing more than to be with you has a fully formed man," he said. "Yet I understand your doubts. If I was in your place, I'm not sure of what I would do. Whatever you choose, I will abide by it."

Shangé pulled Mijoga close

"You are worth losing the heavens for," she said.

"And you are worth losing my being," Mijoga replied.

* * *

Mijoga was gone when she awoke the next morning. She dressed then joined the others for the morning meal. Abasa was the first to speak.

"We will reach the temple today and the priests will be expecting us. There was no way we could approach in secret with the nyama amassed. They will station their warriors at the entrance with their elite hidden inside the temple. Harisajiwe, you will lead our attack. You will break through their ranks. Kiden and Kajok will assist you. Once the stairs are clear, Shange, Mijoga and I will enter the temple and retrieve what we seek."

"How will Mijoga help us?" Shangé asked. "He is in his wild state."

"You won't be able to control him, but he will be there."

"But he might be killed," she said.

"You all might die," Abasa said. "It is the risk you take for freedom from your mutations. I may be able to raise you once I have what I need but I cannot guarantee it. This has never been done before."

Everyone nodded in agreement except Shangé. The closer they came to completing their task the less confident she was in Abasa. But she could not let down the others nor take from Mijoga the chance to be a man again. All her instincts told her this was wrong, but her emotions would not let her speak out. The chance of having Mijoga as himself was too strong.

Kiden flew ahead of the group as they made their way along the circuitous road, following the hills and valleys leading to the temple. After half a day's walk Kiden appeared, landing in front of them.

"The temple is beyond the next hill," she said. "There are twenty guards at the base of the hill. A few villages are scattered about, mostly the women and children of the guards and the priests, I suspect."

"Good," Abasa replied. "Maybe they are not expecting us."

"Then let it be done," Harisajiwe blurted. "The sooner we're finish the sooner I'll be back to my normal self, and I can be rid of you all!"

Harisajiwe sprinted down the road.

"Wait!" Abasa called out, but the stone woman was almost out of sight. Shangé took chase. She was not going to let the woman face whatever lay ahead alone, even though she felt it was all wrong. The road before her tumbled into a deep valley. The hill was further ahead, the land around it cleared of bush. Harisajiwe was almost to the temple, the guards converging toward her. For a moment Shangé thought the stone woman would be able to take the temple on her own until more warriors rushed from the villages and from the temple innards. Harisajiwe plunged into the horde, bodies flying in every direction from the impact. She flailed with her arms, knocking warriors down and away as she strode up the temple stairs. A shrill cry drew Shangé's eyes overhead. What she saw astonished her. Kiden flew down into the valley, carrying Kajok in her claws. The duo swooped at the converging warriors until Kajok's feet were only inches above their heads. She dropped him into their midst and Kajok bellowed before swinging his head from side to side. The stunned warriors fell away momentarily then attacked. Kiden circled the battle, diving into the throng and using her claws to drive back any warrior that came too close to Kajok.

Shange's pace slowed as she watched the battle play out. A grim realization came to her; they were not going to survive. There were too many warriors and they were too well trained.

"You are correct," Abasa said.

The sorcerer stood beside her, his face calm despite the desperate drama unfolding before him. Shangé began to run but Abasa grasped her shoulder. Her legs stiffened and her arms fell to her side.

"Not yet," he said.

"But they will die!" Shangé shouted.

"Yes, they will," Abasa said. "Would you rather it be you?"

"This is wrong!"

"This is necessary," Abasa said. "They knew the risk before they joined me. They knew they might die. Still, they were willing to follow me in hopes that I could change them."

"They did not know they would be sacrificed!"

"No, they did not," Abasa said. "If there was any other way, I would have taken it. But what is their sacrifice compared to all the good I will do for others once I possess the nyama inside?"

"I won't help you," Shangé said.

"You will," Abasa replied. "For if you don't you will lose Mijoga. His wild self will take over and he will disappear into the bush. I cannot restore him to the man you wish him to be unless I possess what's inside that temple."

Shangé watched the battle unfold. Harisajiwe had killed the temple guards and ran to help Kiden and Kajok. Kiden was earthbound, standing beside Kajok and fighting with all she had. Both were bleeding profusely. Shangé prayed they would survive; Kiden collapsed and Kajok threw his body over her. The warriors plunged their spears and swords into the duo until Harisajiwe reached them and began breaking them apart. The warriors rallied around the stone woman, pressing their attack. Harisajiwe's stone-like skin succumbed to the countless blows and blood spurted from her wounds. The sight of her own blood seemed to push her anger higher and her attack redoubled. Soon it was only Harisajiwe and one warrior. The warrior charged the stone woman with his spear; Harisajiwe slapped the weapon aside then gripped the man's neck with both hands. The man clawed as she choked the life from him. His arms fell to his sides and his body went slack. Harisajiwe kept her grip a moment longer before releasing the warrior. He fell to the ground dead. Harisajiwe let loose an ear-piercing cry, shuddered, and then fell on top of him.

Abasa removed his hand from Shangé's shoulder. Feeling came back to her legs. She immediately spun to face Abasa, both swords drawn.

"You know what will happen if you kill me," he said.

Shangé held her blades high for a moment longer before lowering them. Abasa smiled.

"Our reward waits," he said.

Abasa proceeded down the hill and Shangé followed. The sorcerer strolled through the dead without a glance. Shangé stopped at the bodies of the Kaden, Kajok and Harisajiwe, overwhelmed by her shame. She could have helped them, yet she let them fight alone so she could have Mijoga. She said a prayer, hoping her words would ease their passage into the afterlife. She would pour libations for them later, hoping they found in the spirit world what eluded them in the material.

She climbed the steps to the temple entrance. The mausoleum was devoid of any decorations, the paint long faded away, the tapestries that once adorned the walls disintegrated with time. All that remained was a simple white marble tomb resting atop a granite dais. Abasa stood at the base, looking at her expectedly. Shangé trudged to the tomb, and then glared into Abasa's eyes.

"Open it," he ordered.

Shangé placed her hands on the marble then jerked them away. Instead of cold stone she felt warmth and movement. She touched the tomb again and it throbbed in rhythm to her pulse.

"This is not right," she said.

Abasa's eyes narrowed. "Remember why you are here."

The mausoleum echoed with Mijoga's roar. She turned to see her companion saunter into the temple and their eyes met. He was there, but only barely. With no other choice she gripped the edge of the tomb then pushed. The lid fought her; she braced her feet then pushed harder. The lid budged but still resisted. Shangé took a deep breath then pushed again. The lid slid aside, an eerie light escaping its confines. Shangé looked into the tomb. An orb of light pulsed, cradled by silk blankets. She reached into the tomb then picked up the orb. The sensation coursing through her was one she knew from long ago, from a time when her home was the sky and she looked down on those she now lived among. She knew what she had to do.

"You do not deserve this," she said to Abasa. "You are not worthy of it."

The energy bolt from Abasa's hands struck her unaware. The pain was like nothing she'd ever felt and she screamed as she dropped the orb. Mijoga roared then ran to her side. She felt him nuzzle against her body, but she knew he could not help her. She looked on with blurred vision as Abasa knelt and picked up the orb, a victorious smile on his face. Mijoga roared and Abasa extended his hand.

"No Mijoga," she said, her voice barely a whisper. "One of us must live."

"That won't happen," Abasa said.

As Abasa raised his hand the orb transformed. The light dimmed and the object's color became a deep red shade. Abasa stared hungrily at the sphere as he drew it closer, cradling it like a babe. He looked into Shangé's eyes, a malevolent smile on his face.

"Thank you, Shangé," he said. He pushed the orb against his chest, and it melted into his body. Abasa threwwhis head back, his mouth agape as his body took the hue of the orb. For a moment he shimmered, then solidified. When Abasa looked at her again, his eyes blazed like a raging fire.

"Behold your new god!" he said.

Shangé drew her swords. She had no idea what Abasa had become, but she knew he should not exist. Mijoga brushed against her and she looked down. He was fully aware and ready to help her. Sadness touched her briefly as she thought of what might have been.

Abasa's laughed broke her thoughts.

"You think you can stand against me?"

Shangé crouched lower.

"I will try," she replied.

"You will die," Abasa said.

"We shall see."

Abasa spread his arms. The red aura flowed to his hands, forming brilliant orbs in his palms. The spheres elongated and mutated until they became two swords

Abasa sneered. "Shall we?"

The sorcerer closed the distance with such speed that Shangé barely blocked his attack. Flames flashed as their weapons met, the heat searing Shangé's hands. She had to avoid contact with them and try to strike. Mijoga lunged at Abasa; the sorcerer swiped at the simba's head, his sword brushing his mane and setting it aflame. Mijoga howled as he rolled, attempting the put out the fire. Shangé could not reach him; it was taking her all her effort to keep Abasa at bay.

"You will lose," Abasa said. "You are the final sacrifice. Once I take your life the transformation will be complete."

Shangé struggled, dodging Abasa's flaming blades, spurred on by Mijoga's pain-filled roars. She was weak, weaker than she ever felt before but she would not yield. She would not be a sacrifice; she would not let Mijoga die.

The frustration on Abasa's face gave her some satisfaction. They continued to duel, the sun setting on the horizon as darkness crept into the temple. Abasa maneuvered between her and Mijoga and she saw her wounded lover sprawled on the temple floor barely moving. She paid dearly for the distraction. Abasa's sword grazed her right thigh, burning her flesh. She fell to her knees and dropped her swords as she reached for the wound.

"Die!" Abasa shouted.

He lunged for her then jerked still. Mijoga had managed to sink his teeth into Abasa's leg. As the sorcerer struggled Shangé grabbed her swords. Abasa finally kicked free of Mijoga's maw then spun into Shangé's blades. She screamed as she drove them through his chest, then let them go as she fell to the ground. Abasa's shocked face went flat as he collapsed. Shangé watched the red illumination that filled him ooze from his wound then hover over his corpse. It solidified into a human shape, bright balls of fire appearing where eyes would be.

"Who are you?" it asked in a voice that reverberated between the temple walls.

"I am Shangé," she answered.

"Why did you disturb my sleep?" it asked.

"It was not me. It was him."

Shangé nodded at Abasa's body and the being looked upon it.

"He wished power he did not deserve," it said. "What do you wish?"

"I wish to be human," she replied. "And I wish the same for my lover Mijoga."

The being turned its head to look upon Mijoga.

"I cannot grant your wish," it said. "Those that you serve are too powerful for me to challenge . . . for now."

"Then heal us," Shangé pleaded. "If it is in your power do to so."

The being nodded. "That I can do."

It glided to Mijoga then brushed his mane with its hands and the hair became as it was. It ran its hands along his body, the burned skin and bruises dissipating. It then drifted to her, repeating its gestures. Warm pleasure surged through her body as the being repaired her skin and bruises.

"What about the others?" Shangé said.

"I cannot help them," it replied. "They are far beyond this world."

The being's eyes looked upward.

"I must go," it said.

"Wait," Shangé said. "Why did you help us?"

"Because you brought me a sacrifice," it said. It glanced at Abasa's body.

The being rose into the sky, dispersing into the dawn's light. Shangé looked into the heavens for a moment, then hurried to Mijoga. Their eyes met and she knew he was still inside. She sat beside him, hugging his neck and burying her face into his mane.

"We must be more careful," she said. "Hope made us careless."

Mijoga let out a small roar.

Shangé stood then gathered her weapons. She took one last look at Abasa's corpse then walked away from the temple in the morning light. Mijoga followed.

ABOUT THE AUTHOR

Milton Davis is an award winning Black Speculative fiction writer and owner of MVmedia, LLC, a publishing company specializing in Science Fiction and Fantasy based on African/African Disapora history, culture and traditions. Milton is the author of twenty-one novels and short story collections; his most recent the Sword and Soul adventure *Eda Blessed II*. Milton is also a contributing author to Black Panther: Tales of Wakanda, published by Marvel and Titan Books *and coauthor of Hadithi and the State of Black Speculative Fiction* with Eugen Bacon. He is the editor and co-editor of ten anthologies; *Terminus: Tales of the Black Fantastic from the ATL*; *Cyberfunk!*; *The City, Dark Universe* and *Dark Universe: The Bright Empire* with Gene Peterson; *Griots: A Sword and Soul Anthology and Griot: Sisters of the Spear*, with Charles R. Saunders; *The Ki Khanga Anthology*, the *Steamfunk! Anthology*, and the *Dieselfunk!*

anthology with Balogun Ojetade. Milton's work had also been featured in *Black Power: The Superhero Anthology and Rococoa published by Roaring Lions Productions*; Skelos *2: The Journal of Weird Fiction and Dark Fantasy, Steampunk Writers Around the World* published by Luna Press; *Heroika: Dragoneaters* published by First Perseid Press, Bass *Reeves Frontier Marshal Volume Two*, and *Slay: Stories of the Vampire Noire*. Milton Davis and Balogun Ojetade won the 2014 Urban Action Showcase Award for Best Script. Milton's story 'The Swarm' was nominated for the 2017 British Science Fiction Association Award for Short Fiction and his story, Carnival, has been nominated for the 2020 British Science Fiction Association Award for Short Fiction.

Shange and Mijoga find themselves aiding a desperate village whose inhabitants are disappearing during the night. What they find takes them deep into the bowels of the earth to confront an ancient and bloodthirsty evil.

The Blood Seekers. A Shangé and Mijoga graphic novel by Milton J. Davis and Kristopher Michael Mosby. Available at MVmedia, LLC. www.mvmediaatl.com

Printed in the USA
CPSIA information can be obtained
at www.ICGtesting.com
LVHW010832100424
776593LV00011B/155

9 781737 227762